If ever in your life you are faced
with a choice, a difficult decision,
a quandary,

Ask yourself,
"What would Edgar and Ellen do?"

And do exactly the contrary.

Edgar & Ellen

HOT AIR

Edgar & Ellen

# HOT AIR

by
**CHARLES OGDEN**

*illustrations by*
**RICK CARTON**

**ALADDIN**
New York   London   Toronto   Sydney

Watch out for Edgar & Ellen in:

*Rare Beasts*        *Nod's Limbs*
*Tourist Trap*
*Under Town*        *Edgar & Ellen*
*Pet's Revenge*      *Mischief Manual*
*High Wire*

❦ ALADDIN
An imprint of Simon & Schuster Children's Publishing Division
1230 Avenue of the Americas, New York, NY 10020
Text and illustrations copyright © 2008 by Star Farm Productions, LLC
All rights reserved, including the right of reproduction in whole or in part in any form.
ALADDIN and related logo are registered trademarks of Simon & Schuster, Inc.

Designed by Star Farm Productions, LLC.
The text of this book was set in Bembo, Auldroon, and Lettres Eclatees.
The illustrations in this book were rendered in pen and ink and digitally enhanced in Photoshop.
Manufactured in the United States of America
First Aladdin edition August 2008
10   9   8   7   6   5   4   3   2   1

Library of Congress Cataloging-in-Publication Data
Ogden, Charles.
Hot air / by Charles Ogden ; illustrated by Rick Carton. — 1st Aladdin ed.
p.  cm. — (Edgar & Ellen)
Summary: When the founder of the town of Nod's Limbs returns after a two hundred year absence, trouble-making twins Edgar and Ellen attempt to discover who is trying to steal the secret that kept him alive all that time, while they also scheme to sabotage the town's mayoral election.
ISBN-13: 978-1-4169-5465-1 (paper over board)
ISBN-10: 1-4169-5465-1 (paper over board)
[1. Twins—Fiction. 2. Brothers and sisters—Fiction. 3. Politics, Practical—Fiction. 4. Humorous stories. 5. Mystery and detective stories.] I. Carton, Rick, ill. II. Title.
PZ7.O333Ho 2008
[Fic]—dc22
2007029825

HERE IS MY DEDICATION—

—CHARLES

## SO VENTURE FORTH DOWN UNTROD STREETS...

## It Begins Anew . . .

A chorus of chipper birdies (wide-bottom chicka-dees, ruby-tufted prairie sparrows, and possibly a whiskered marsh finch or two) heralded the impending sunrise with a .urry of merry *too-too-wit*s and *chee-chee-weet*s. Dawn was coming to Nod's Limbs, and like most dawns in this happy little town, it was sure to be glorious.

But the pleasant birdsongs stopped in midtweet at a harsh clanking in the darkness. Somewhere out there, someone was uncoiling heavy chains.

"Careful, Sister! You're throwing us off balance!"

"Oh, *I* am? Maybe *you* should adjust your steer-ing, Brother!"

Several of the birds (notably the yellow-bellied wren, a jittery species) flew off as something large and slow brushed against the treetops, blotting out the scant light of the crescent moon.

Low voices hissed in the darkness.

"Steady as she goes, Brother. We're almost overhead."

"That's *Captain Edgar* to you, sailor."

"Then you may call me Admiral Ellen, *sailor*. Now, full stop! Time to go to work."

More clanking of chains ensued. If any curious bird remained, it would have made no sense of this bloated thing in the nighttime sky, resembling, as it did, a blackened ball of seed, or a shadowy glob of suet. Odder still was the sight of the young girl descending from it on a length of chain. This girl crawled down, down, down until she alit upon the roof of one of the many covered bridges that spanned the Running River. Scrambling across it, she encircled the bridge with the chain, again and again, wrapping the structure (as it must have appeared to the birds) as a spider prepares a fly for dinner. She padlocked the links of the chains together securely and whistled sharply.

"Hit it, Cap'n!"

Above the treetops, hideous torrents of fire erupted in midair. The flame came from the hot-air balloon he piloted, and the red glow illuminated a pale boy wearing striped footie pajamas. The balloon struggled to rise, tethered fast to the bridge below.

"Is that all you've got, Edgar?"

"Not by a long shot! Engaging secondary thrusters now!"

The boy hit a switch, and a pair of belt-driven fan blades blew a gale-force blast straight down. The river water roiled, and the long grass on the banks lay flat under the wind. The girl clung desperately onto the chain, flapping like a wind sock.

With a creak, a groan, and a long, baleful moan, the bridge released its grip on the earth and came swinging free. Another burst of hot flames, and the balloon lurched upward, carrying the bridge with it.

"We did it!" exclaimed the girl, climbing into the basket.

"And not a moment too soon," said the boy. "Here come our first commuters!"

From the north, a pair of headlights trundled down Copenhagen Lane. From the south, one headlight and the sound of squeaky pedals crept northward. The two vehicles—one a dairy truck, the other a newspaper boy's bike—slowed as they neared the spot where the bridge used to be. They stopped at opposite banks of the Running River.

High above them, the boy whispered, "They're really going to flip their wigs!"

A sturdy woman in a neat, white uniform leaned out of the delivery truck. She scratched her head.

"Clovis, is that you?" she called across the river.

"Yes, Miss Miller," replied the newspaper boy.

"Clovis, isn't there usually a bridge here?"

"Yes, Miss Miller."

Just then, a Baltimore maudlin-throated raven, tired from a night of pestering a local statuary, perched upon the bridge's roof and let loose its famous late-night call: *Nevva-moo! Nevva-moo!*

"Why, that sounds like the first Baltimore maudlin of the season," said the dairy worker, looking up. "What the—? Lookie here, Clovis! Our bridge has flown the coop!"

The pair in the balloon held their breaths as the people below craned their necks skyward, catching this blatant feat of mischief in the act.

"Edgar and Ellen!" bellowed the dairy driver. "This is . . . this is . . . the *best prank yet*!"

"Yeah, hilarious!" cried the newsboy. "Wait

till I tell everyone on my route about this! What a hoot!"

"Keep up the good work!" they called as the balloon floated off into the distance with the purloined bridge.

The twins in the balloon glanced at each other with slightly confused expressions.

"They didn't exactly flip their wigs," said Edgar.

"No, not really," said Ellen. "They sort of enjoyed it."

"Still, they're right: This *is* our best prank yet. Unparalleled success, no question . . ."

"I suppose."

But as the twins leaned on the edges of their balloon basket, only the Baltimore maudlin was close enough to hear them mutter: "So why wasn't it more fun?"

## 1. The Most Pleasant Town in the World

If you had grown up in the charming town of Nod's Limbs, you probably would have been extremely happy. After all, everybody else in Nod's Limbs is extremely happy, and that sort of thing is contagious, like a head cold or a yawn.

Nestled into lush, green hills on the banks of the Running River, the town looked more pleasant than the prettiest postcard. True, the Running River was not much more than a creek, and the trees on those green hills were occasionally blighted by nests of cuckoo wasps. But all in all, everything about the place was utterly delightful.

Delightful to a point, however. For—it must be mentioned—things had become wondrous strange in recent months, ever since the day town founder Augustus Nod had walked out of an underground cavern, alive after two centuries alone in darkness.

In many towns, this event might have been met with disbelief, but not so in Nod's Limbs. Here, townsfolk found it easier to simply accept this marvel without getting bogged down by questions such as "Shouldn't he be dead?" and "What miraculous substance could have kept him alive all those years?"

With these complex and worrisome questions safely ignored, the citizenry could concentrate on what they did best: celebrating. And celebrate they did. The town's new motto, "Everything Nod Is New Again!" manifested itself everywhere: Nod's original candle factory, the Waxworks, was being restored to its former glory; Rickets Road had been renamed Augustus Avenue; ice cream vendors sold Chocolate-Covered Nod Pops from their pushcarts; and Augie was fast becoming the most popular name for both baby boys *and* girls.

Change was afoot in other ways, too. The mayoral family, who had ruled in a continuous chain since Nod's time, had been disgraced and banished the day the old man reemerged. Now, for the first time in the history of Nod's Limbs, the upcoming mayoral election had more than one name on the ballot, and neither of them was Knightleigh.

Odd, too, was the town's new attitude toward the practice of mischief. In years past, when something went awry—such as a giant pitcher of maple syrup spilling over the town, or jet turbines blowing a blizzard of confetti through the business district—the citizens did their best not to question it. The less said about these unseemly events, they reasoned, the sooner life could return to normal.

These days, however, the townsfolk had a new definition for "normal." A new spirit had come over them, a spirit of merry misbehavior and mischievous monkeyshines.

Most likely this new attitude could be blamed on Nod's return—for, after all, how *should* one react when madmen walk the earth centuries after being given up for dead? How *should* one react when cherished civic leaders prove to be liars, thieves, and would-be murderers? How *should* one react when the entire status quo is flipped upside down? In Nod's Limbs the answer was this: accept it. After all, one could continue to seek a *normal life*, as long as "normal" meant that covered bridges sometimes went aloft.

As Edgar and Ellen were revealed that day to be the driving force behind most of the mischief the town had ever experienced, the twins were elevated quite logically from "irregular nuisances" to "status quo."

And the status quo was something to be taken very seriously in a town like Nod's Limbs.

## 2. The Heroes of Nod's Limbs

Edgar pulled his jester cap down firmly upon his head as he and Ellen traipsed into town.

"Ready for a great day of pranking, Sister?"

"Of course, Brother," said Ellen, who wore a similar headpiece. The bells on their caps jangled jarringly in the peaceful morning air. "Another Tuesday, another parade. What do we celebrate today?"

"Prank You Very Much Day," said Edgar. "And we will rule supreme, as always. Heimertz and Dahlia built our float from my designs. It's really going to knock 'em for a loop!"

As they neared Town Hall, they could see a spectacle of floats and banners and balloons. The marching band tuned up at top volume. As the twins made their way, adoring fans accosted them on every side with hearty handshakes and slaps on the back.

"Edgar and Ellen! Edgar and Ellen!" cried a group of children. To a one they were dressed in red and white footie pajamas (although theirs were markedly less filthy than the twins').

"How do you like our new uniforms?" asked Donald Bogginer. "As president of the official Edgar and Ellen Fan Club, I ordered a pair for every member."

"Er, nice . . . but a little too tidy," said Ellen doubtfully.

"Will you still be holding your mischief class tonight?" Donald continued. "Last week's class, How to Give Presents to Edgar and Ellen, was sure insightful, but some of us are ready to learn something a little more, you know, mischievous."

Edgar snickered. "All in good time, Bogginer. Tonight you will be unwrapping all the chocolates that get showered upon us during this parade, then feeding them to us as you fan us with palm leaves!"

"Uh . . . neat!" said Donald. "I guess that's kind of mischievous."

"Of course it is!" said Ellen. "Now off with you. Go put bananas in the tubas or something."

The eyes of their fans widened, and they turned and fled at once.

The twins finally made it to their float, which was shaped and decorated like an enormous mound of half-digested food.

"Isn't it something?" said Edgar.

"Is vomit really a prank? Ellen asked.

Edgar rubbed his hands. "Just you wait!"

Ronan Heimertz, the caretaker of the twins' house, stepped out from behind the float. He smiled broadly, like he always did, and patted the float proudly.

"You've outdone yourself, Heimertz," said Edgar. "Great rotten-egg impersonation, Pet!" he called up to the hairy creature that sat atop the float. Although Pet wore no costume, its single yellow eye did look very much like a rotten egg. Pet waved a tendril back at the twins.

"Yes, and I love the use of gastroberries for the peas," said Ellen. "They really give it that authentic barfy feel."

"Thank you. I try to pick perfect flowers for to decorate," said Madame Dahlia, who emerged from a mound of stinkweed grasses and muck bush on the float's platform. She gazed warmly down at Heimertz, who reached up to stroke her big toe. "But why we wait? Hurry, onto float! The parade soon start!"

With that, Heimertz picked each twin up by the pajama neck, as if they weighed no more than a skunk orchid (several of which lined the sides of the float, looking remarkably like half-digested licorice), and deposited them onto the platform. Then he vaulted himself up and took his place next to Madame Dahlia. He gently took her hand and kissed it.

"Blech," said Ellen.

"Ahoy there, are we ready to roll?" Bob, the interim mayor, strode up to the float, making a check mark on his clipboard.

"Ready to show this town what real pranking looks like," said Edgar.

"That's all we ask," said Bob. He thrust out his hand for a handshake. "Put 'er there, pal!"

"Bob . . . that's a handshake buzzer in your hand," said Ellen. "I can see it."

"Ah! Can't fool you, can I?" said Bob. "Hey, do you want a peanut from this generic-looking can?"

An airhorn blast in the distance signaled the beginning of the parade. Bob waved as the twin's float lurched out from behind its curtains.

Although marred by the expected lame prank attempts of citizens along the parade route ("Why do they always think we'll fall for the 'your shoelace is untied' gag?" asked Ellen, waving her pajama footie), the spectacle delivered, in every way a Nod's Limbs spectacle should: loud brass music, cheering children on their parents' shoulders, a steady shower of streamers and confetti, and especially a torrent of chocolates and caramels falling on Edgar and Ellen, as usual.

Ellen leaned close to Edgar. "Brother, do you feel at all strange about this? I mean, leading all the parades and teaching mischief classes and, crud, they're dressing like us and acting like us. Just a little while ago we wanted nothing to do with these people."

"That was before we knew how much they *needed* us," Edgar whispered back. "We bring the fun, Sister. Yeah, they've got some catching up to do, but as long as they're pelting me with candy and gifts, I'll be their hero. Now put your back into that wave."

As the floats came to a stop at the end of the parade route, a crush of celebrating citizens milled about, waving flags and cheering the floats. Edgar chuckled and pressed a red button under his seat. A sinister ticking came from the float beneath them.

"Attention, my subjects!" Edgar shouted to the crowd. "It's been another wonderful and pranky parade. But now I give you the best prank of them all—Operation: Blow Chunk!"

As the twins dove under their float, the top erupted like an angry volcano, coating the assembled masses in yellow slime and hunks of rancid gelatin. In the silence that followed, Edgar and Ellen could hear only the sickening squish of goo dripping off their victims. At last, Betty LaFete broke the silence:

"Well! Another amazing prank," she said. "A bit . . . uh, stinky, but still a laugh and a half, wouldn't you say, Buffy?"

"Oh, sure," said Buffy, proprietor of Buffy's Muffins. "Quite, um, impressive. I'm going to need another shower today—seems a bit wasteful of water—but all in the name of good fun, right, fellow citizens?"

A smattering of claps and half-hearted cheers went

up through the crowd. Edgar and Ellen smiled and waved in victory. They couldn't hear the grumbles that came from the back.

"They call that funny?" said executive business executive Marvin Matterhorn. "What's funny about sticky loafers?"

"Nothing, that's what," said mayoral candidate Eugenia Smithy, wiping yellow goo from her eyes. "When I win this election, that will be the end of unexpected events like this!"

Still, the twins didn't detect the slightest displeasure from their escapade, and stomped through the mess, singing a song of triumph:

> *The future is a funny thing;*
> *No one can say what it will bring.*
> *Who ever thought Nod's Limbs would ring*
> *Us in as mischief queen and king?*
> *So launch that candy! Cheer our names!*
> *Praise us for our pranking games!*
> *We've reached the pinnacle of fame,*
> *And life will never be the same!*
> *Still, it is a little weird*
> *That now we're loved instead of feared.*

## 3. The Old Man

Edgar and Ellen returned home to their mansion. It was not the same house they had lived in their entire lives; that monument to misdeeds had fallen down the day Nod emerged from underground. Still, an exact duplicate existed: the Knightlorian Hotel, which, like most of former mayor Knightleigh's possessions, returned to Nod's ownership upon his reappearance. The hotel had been built as a mirror opposite of the twins' home—eleven floors of pristine and pretty perfection. But with a little hard work and perseverance, the twins had brought about an air of dingy decay the building sorely lacked.

Edgar and Ellen now rode the elevator to the tenth floor, the highest bedroom in town with undoubtedly the best view for plotting, planning, and percolating new ideas. Instead of doing any of those things, though, they unloaded their sacks of candy and, unwilling to wait for their fan club, devoured every sweet treat in sight. With bellies swollen and mouths crusted in chocolate, they flopped onto their beds, moaning.

Just then, a voice boomed over the intercom: "Children! In my study! At once!"

"Uh-oh—the old man," said Edgar.

"Not now." Ellen groaned. "My whole body has a tummyache."

"Children! No lollygagging!" thundered the voice over the intercom.

The twins pulled themselves together and loped to the elevators. Edgar paused before pressing the down button. "Tradition or custom?" he asked.

"Better not keep him waiting."

"Custom it is, then."

Edgar pulled an umbrella handle from a nearby potted plant (a thriving *Nosferatus morticia* in full bloom) and pried open the elevator doors. The empty elevator shaft loomed before them. Ellen kicked a panel in the wall, and it slid aside to reveal two pairs of odd-looking metal boots. The twins slipped on the oversized footwear.

"Countersink boots, go!" they cried as they leaped. For a moment the twins plummeted into the blackness of the elevator shaft, but then a powerful stream of compressed air blasted from the soles of the boots, slowing their fall to a slightly less deadly speed.

When they floated near the fifth floor, Edgar opened the elevator doors with a touch of a lever. But he bumped into Ellen, and their legs became tangled.

Suddenly the thrusting air of the countersink boots was no longer gently slowing their fall, but rocketing them forcefully into the fifth-floor hallway. They tumbled head over footies like red-and-gray-striped bowling balls, through the door of the old man's study.

*KRRRAK!*

The door splintered and the twins landed in a heap in front of the desk. The boots sputtered and coughed as they ran out of their last puffs of air.

A man with long, gray hair sat behind the desk, scribbling furiously into a fat, leather-bound journal. He didn't even look up. "That is the third door this month."

"Yes, Nod."

"Sorry, Nod."

"And every time you use those confounded boots, you cost me seven hundred dollars in fuel refills."

"Aw, Nod," said Edgar, pulling himself from the heap, "that's chump change for us bazillionaires."

Augustus Nod slammed the book shut. "This bazillionaire intends to *stay* a bazillionaire, you ungrateful— What on Earth do you have on your faces?"

"Huh? Oh, chocolate," said Ellen. "From today's festival."

"Ah, yes." Nod scowled. "Why you persist in encouraging that town's hero worship is quite beyond me."

"Nod, what part of 'chocolate' don't you understand?" said Edgar.

"I fear you're treading the primrose path of dalliance," growled Nod.

"We're what?" said Ellen.

"Shakespeare." Nod sighed. "By which I mean, 'Don't be led astray.' Anyway, we have things to discuss. Take your seats, please."

Edgar and Ellen pulled up two high-backed chairs and, as was their habit in Nod's study, inspected the cushions before sitting. They each discovered one plump, red, rubber bag hidden beneath the fabric.

"Whoopee cushions, Nod?" asked Ellen. "A little unimaginative for you, isn't it?"

Nod heaved a sigh. "Perhaps. These days, my little charges, I don't seem to have the . . . the . . . Oh, how do they say it in the modern age? The bandstand? Yes, the bandstand for details."

"Uh, Nod?" said Edgar. "I think you mean band-*width*."

"Confound this future babble," said Nod. "I just can't seem to get the hinge of it!"

"The *hang* of it," said Ellen. "It's okay, Nod. Two hundred years alone is bound to take the edge off your language skills."

"Perhaps. Or perhaps I'm once again devoting too much time to researching the balm."

*The balm.* Nod leaned over and patted the battered bucket that held no more than a couple gallons of the smelly goop, which had kept him alive so long underground—and which had nourished Pet back to full, feisty health. It was their only remaining supply of the substance; Ellen had managed to carry two buckets out of Nod's underground prison as it collapsed around them, but after their harrowing escape only one bucket survived. Nod estimated that there was enough balm in the bucket to feed Pet comfortably for another several decades. If he knew how long it would continue to sustain his own life, however, Nod kept mum about it.

"Yes, old habits are hard to break," said Nod. "Now that I know I'm not the only one who knows about this potent substance, I fear its power could be exploited, misused."

Nod stole a glance out the window, as if sinister forces were lurking in the forest outside.

"Relax, Nod, that's what the circus folk are for," said Ellen. "The Heimertz family is out there protecting balm springs all over the world from kooks and power-hungry nut jobs."

"That band of acrobats and sideshow freaks is a formidable force not even *I* want to tangle with," added Edgar. "As long as they're on the job, no one will ever discover the balm's powers."

"Yes, the balm's powers," said Nod dreamily. "Oh, how I yearn to crack those secrets. I've been corresponding with Ringmaster Benedict, comparing notes, analyzing data and hypotheses . . ." Nod's voice began to trail off. "Of course, at lower temperatures, its ill effects might intensify . . . Perhaps I could offset that with a tincture of borodinium. . . ."

"Nod, wake up!" barked Ellen. "You're starting to sound like the kind of person the circus is protecting the balm from."

Nod snapped to attention. "Quite right. You see why I fear for its security. The prospect of its life-extending abilities—and other effects undreamed of!—is far too alluring for lesser men." He pounded his fist on the desk. "Enough. You don't care about that. You're interested in why I called you: We've got to finalize our plans for the wedding."

"The wedding! Oh, right," said Edgar. "Well, I've drawn up blueprints for ejector springs to be installed in Heimertz's dress shoes. Right in the middle of the ceremony—*sproing!*"

"And I've nearly finished training Dahlia's gaseous flytraps," said Ellen. "Give me a few more days, and they should belch on command during the vows."

"Excellent plans, both," replied Nod gruffly. "However, since the wedding is first thing tomorrow morning, I see they will go unfulfilled."

"Tomorrow?" said Edgar. "How did we miss that?"

"Perhaps you've taken your duties about town too seriously," harrumphed Nod.

"Well, tell me *you* at least have something devious planned for this wedding," said Ellen.

"I was counting on you two. I've been distracted by this latest letter from Benedict. He proposes some unsettling theories. . . ," Nod trailed off again. "Of course, if I could replicate the exact frigid conditions, I could see if the mitosis process remained constant. . . ."

"Hello? Earth to Nod!" said Ellen.

Nod shook his head. "Why would the planet be calling me? Ellen, are these more of your mind toys?"

"Mind *games*," said Ellen. "And no. You were lost in thought again."

"I'm not lost!" said Nod. "I know right where I am at all times! And who can concentrate on weddings when there are perilous mysteries still to be unlocked in the balm?"

"Easy, Nod," said Edgar. "There's nothing to worry about. The Knightleigh family was our only threat in this town, and they've been completely *crushed*."

"That's right," Ellen boasted. "They're penniless and their reputation is ruined. No Knightleigh will ever be mayor in this town again."

"You vanquished the ruling mayoral family, Nod," Edgar pointed out. "They had treated this place as their personal playground for two hundred years. You've got back all your wealth from them, and now you're on easy street with two of the town's most adorable tricksters on your team—"

"I am *not* adorable, Edgar."

"Too true, Ellen. Too true. But try telling that to our fan club. Donald Bogginer *obviously* has a crush on you."

"Edgar, do not let other children crush your sister," admonished Nod. "Now, you should be off; prepare as best you can for the wedding. Oh, and one last thing: I may be distracted, but I'm not *completely* out of ideas. . . ."

Nod dove under his desk. The twins glanced at the whoopee cushions in their laps. The red, rubber bags were swelling like baking biscuits.

"Molasses bombs?" said Edgar. "Nod, you foul—"

*Ker-BLAMMO!*

Nod tittered fiendishly from the molasses-free zone beneath his desk.


## 4. For Whom the Wedding Bell Tolls

One minute after sunrise (according to Heimertz Family Circus tradition), Edgar threw open the door to the ninth-floor ballroom. He wore an oversized tuxedo, and Ellen tripped along behind in the mint green dress Dahlia had made for her. Both of them had their footie pajamas beneath their outfits, but they fulfilled their promise to Nod to look the part for the wedding.

"Oh, my precious Ellen! You look beautiful as blooming *Toxico pernicius!*"

Ellen grimaced as Dahlia entered the room, arms wide. Those arms—strengthened by years of taming vicious plants for the circus—seized Ellen in a hug that squeezed the breath from her lungs.

"*T-toxico pernicius* d-doesn't bloom, Dahlia," gasped Ellen.

"Correct. You are most good student to pass such tricky test." Dahlia laughed. "You like dress I sew you, yes? Make you look so much a young woman! Maybe I sew more for school? One dress for each day of school week?"

Ellen extracted herself from Dahlia's arms. "Um, why don't you finish my botany lessons first. I, uh, need those more."

"Spoken like my best pupil," said the plant tamer.

Dahlia herself was dressed in a handmade sea green wedding gown with a slim band of blue jewels sewn down one side of the dress to accentuate her long figure. Her childlike joy shone as bright as a bouquet of iridescent moonflowers.

A dozen flattering remarks ticked through Ellen's brain, but she quickly dismissed each one. Ellen was not a girl accustomed to paying compliments. She could not hide her genuine smile, however, and Dahlia read her mind.

"Thank you, Ellen."

Across the room, near a humble makeshift altar, Edgar approached a very nervous Nod.

"Nice threads, old man," Edgar said. Nod stopped pacing and made a slight bow. He was dressed in tails, and top hat, looking every bit the nineteenth-century gentleman. He had obtained his justice-of-the-peace license specifically for this occasion, and was taking a last-minute thumb-through of his copy of *Tying the Knot Tight: A Guide to Not Botching the Big Day.*

"Let's get this over with," called Nod. "I'm ready to booger down."

"*Boogie*, Nod, *boogie*," corrected Edgar.

"Not yet, lad. The ceremony first!"

In another odd bit of circus tradition, it was the groom who walked down the aisle toward his bride. Gustav and Morella, the beloved yet vicious snapping shrubs tended to by Dahlia and Ellen, stood at attention beside the altar as a botanical best man and leafy maid of honor. Nod rose above it all on a wooden platform, speed-reading through his book and mumbling to himself.

Edgar picked up an accordion and squeezed out the opening refrain of the traditional Heimertz family wedding march ("Here Comes the Groom, Give Him Some Room"). On cue with the accordion theme, Pet (in bow tie and tiny top hat) leaped up and pulled open a curtain at the back of the room to reveal the massive boulder of a man standing inside the doorway.

Heimertz wore a powder blue tuxedo with a white frilly shirt beneath. His mustache was waxed and curled, and his white teeth seemed even brighter than usual. Edgar and Ellen were taken aback by their creepy caretaker's transformation. Where once this had been a man they feared—indeed, the only thing they feared—he now stood before them a friend, a hero, and a protector. To be fair, however, the tuxedo was a little tight, causing his ever-present smile to surge a little more sharply across his face, and this was unsettling.

Heimertz lumbered down the aisle, doing an occasional pirouette (more circus tradition). At the altar, he gently took Dahlia's hand in his colossal paw and looked into her eyes. He inhaled for what

seemed a very long time, and then rumbled two words in the voice of a living earthquake:

"I do."

"Now, you've gone and skipped ahead," said a flummoxed Nod, flipping through his book. "I've still got some 'dearly beloveds' and a 'forever hold your peace' to get through."

"Never mind, Augustus," said Dahlia. "I do, too."

Pet held a handkerchief to its eye and shed a single— although nonetheless quite enormous—tear.

## 5. Up, Up, and Go Away

After the exchange of rings and the bride and groom's kiss, the wedding party celebrated heartily for the rest of the morning. Nod had ordered a veritable smorgasbord of treats, and the buffet table was stacked high with meats and muffins, cheeses and chilled gelatin squares. Ellen, as a wedding present, had even carved an ice sculpture centerpiece of the bride and groom.

"See, Heimertz, here's you flying out of a cannon, just like in your circus days," she explained.

Edgar cocked an eyebrow. "Which end of this ice lump is Heimertz, Ellen?"

"It's *art*," she sneered, "not a passport photo."

Ronan Heimertz simply smiled and swallowed the tribute whole.

After much eating and dancing and pranking, it was time for the newlyweds to depart and for Nod to reveal his wedding gift. He opened the ballroom window, then gestured for the celebrants to take a look.

"Behold!" he announced. "Your chariot awaits!"

"Uh, Nod, that's not much of a chariot," said Ellen as she leaned out the window. "There's nothing down there."

"*Down*, no," said Nod. "But *up* is another story."

When the party turned their eyes upward, they saw what appeared to be a giant cloud eclipsing

the sun. But this was no cloud. It was a great, gray blimp, moored to the roof of the mansion.

"Oh, Augustus!" cried Dahlia. "A dirigible? For us? You are most kind."

She kissed the old man on his cheek, and the twins could see him blush under his thick beard.

"Enough mush, woman," he sputtered. "It's time for you lovebirds to skedoodle."

"You are meaning *skedaddle*, gentle man," said Dahlia. "And I think I am agreeing. Ronan?"

With that, Ronan Heimertz picked up his new bride and threw her out the window. As any good circus performer would, Dahlia deftly caught hold of the rope ladder that dangled a few feet outside the window. Heimertz quickly leaped after her, and the wedded couple climbed up to their floating transport.

"Good-bye, friends," called Dahlia. "The time has come at last for facing our circus family and patching up past troubles. We will think of you fondly and return soon!"

Ronan waved one last time before ducking into the blimp's carriage and firing up its motor. As the massive flying machine purred away over the tree-tops, Nod heaved a sigh.

"At last, a return to peace and quiet," he said.

But Nod's newfound tranquility lasted a mere seven seconds.

## 6. The Wedding Crusher

*Klong! Klong! Klong! Klongklongklongklongklong!*

"One of our alarms," said Edgar. "Fifth floor!"

"That's my office," said Nod. "Quickly, respond!"

While Nod took the elevator, Edgar, Ellen, and Pet took the faster route: down the fireman's pole to the seventh-floor music parlor, then a quick slide down some ductwork. There, a ship's bell *klong*ed incessantly at them above a complicated snare made of manne-quin arms with spiky-sharp fingernails. The arms had sprung out at someone who was no longer there.

"Escaped the Claptrap?" said Ellen. "How?"

"Fan out," said Edgar. The trio scanned the stairways, landings, and secret passages. But the house was quiet from bottom to top.

By the time they reconvened in Nod's office, the old man was pacing. The room had been ransacked, with papers scattered everywhere and drawers spilled open.

"No one there, Nod," said Edgar. "Whoever it was, we chased him off."

"Chased him off? Or allowed him to escape?" demanded Nod. "We've been burgled, children."

"A thief? In Nod's Limbs?" marveled Ellen.

"What's missing?" asked Edgar.

"Various of my journals, sheafs of papers, the first draft of my autobiography—most of it trash. With one exception." Nod shook with anger. "My letters from Benedict have been taken! All our musings on the balm—It's information of great danger if in the wrong hands!"

"It must just be some kind of prank by an over-zealous Nod's Limbsian," said Ellen. "Right?"

"Oh, really? Then why didn't any of your usual traps deter this fiend, twins?" thundered Nod.

Ellen looked up sheepishly. "Maybe because—"

"I'll tell you why!" cried Nod, picking up a set of droopy bear traps tangled in coils of wire. *"The Tiger Claw Surprise was NEVER reset after the last time a pair of twins MISUSED it in a game of hide, seek, and subdue!"*

Edgar gulped. "Didn't you reset it, Ellen?"

Ellen's eyes bulged. "Me? It's the loser's job to reset the traps!"

"Enough!" yelled Nod. "Twins, you've been sloppy and inattentive, two atrocious qualities for ones who would call themselves pranksters. You can make it up to me by retrieving those letters *immediately.*"

The twins gulped hard.

"I don't wish to alarm you unduly," said Nod, "so I'll say only that the fate of humanity hangs in the balance."

"What?" cried Edgar. "*That's* not alarming us unduly?"

"I'm trying to put it gently!" Nod harrumphed.

"We'll find those letters, Nod," said Ellen. "No one outmischiefs us in this town."

"Not twice in the same day, I hope," growled Nod. The twins winced. "Now, I must communicate with Benedict at once. I will fetch one of the homing ravens. Edgar and Ellen, take Pilos with you and get some results. If you don't, we're all muffins!"

"Er, toast?" offered Edgar.

"No, thank you!" Nod pushed them all out of his study and slammed the door.

## 7. Can You Dig It?

"Unbelievable!" said Ellen.

"Believe it," said Edgar.

"Well, unacceptable, then."

"Agreed. I'm sure you're right, though, that this is some crazed Nod's Limbsian who's delighted he's pulling a fast one on us."

"We can't take chances. We begin with a house-by-house sweep of town," said Ellen. "You take fingerprints, I'll shake down our suspects—"

"Slow down, Sister," said Edgar. "Let's start with some sniffing closer to home."

"Sniff?" Ellen howled. "We should huff, puff, and blow down this whole town until we get our perp!"

"First, we must be detectives," said Edgar, "so let us detect."

Edgar pulled a magnifying glass out of his satchel and handed it to Pet. Edgar stooped to examine the stairs, following Pet as the hairball held the glass for him. They walked in this way for several flights until they got to the basement steps.

"Interesting . . . interesting . . . interesting," Edgar murmured.

"Boring. Boring! *Boring!*" Ellen fumed. "What could the floor possibly tell you that I couldn't get from a living Nod's Limbsian under a spotlight interrogation?"

"Well, my dear sidekick," said Edgar, "this floor is currently telling me our visitor wore boots. See? A faint boot print here on the third step. And do we wear boots, Sister?"

"No," said Ellen. "But it's probably just Nod—"

"Oh, my unobservant assistant. Nod wears ratty old slippers. Heimertz wears boots, true, but at least seven sizes larger than these."

"Big deal. We already knew someone came up the stairs—"

"But what substance did our intruder tread upon?" said Edgar. "This doesn't look like garden mud, does it?"

Ellen leaned in beside Edgar and peeked through the magnifying glass. "Hm. No, the soil around our house is enriched with Muldavian algae moss, making it much redder than this. This print has a gray-green hue and a faint curdled odor, like . . . like . . ."

Ellen gasped.

*"Sewer sludge!"* the twins said in unison.

"Tracked from the basement," said Edgar.

"This can't be," said Ellen. "There's never been sewer access from the basement of this house. . . ."

"Nevertheless," said Edgar, "no matter how unlikely, the evidence suggests otherwise."

Pet hopped into Edgar's hands and held its tendrils in the shape of a hairy arrow pointing down. "I agree," said Edgar. "To the basement!"

With renewed seriousness, the twins scrutinized

the steps leading down to the basement and found more boot prints, in thicker and thicker globs of sewer sludge. The steps to the subbasement were even more obviously marked.

"I still can't believe this," said Ellen. "Did this person wriggle through a sewer pipe?"

"That would require a person of small stature or exceptional agility," said Edgar. "Circus folk, perhaps?"

But the footprints didn't lead to a sewer pipe at all. They stopped cold at a wall.

"Impossible!" said Ellen.

"No, merely improbable," said Edgar. "Even so, here we are. . . ."

The twins ran their hands over the smooth bricks of the subbasement wall, probing for telltale cracks or hidden indentations.

Pet shuffled along the base of the wall, its little hairs whipping about like a whisk broom as it looked for abnormalities. Its pupil widened with alarm when it came level with a narrow hole about two hands high from the floor. The creature traced frantic figure eights around the twins' footies.

"What is it, Pet? Did you find something?"

Pet sidled up to the hole and twirled three greasy strands of hair into a braid. It poked this braid into the hole, and the twins heard a soft *click*.

The entire wall swung up, knocking the twins and Pet backward. The trio rubbed their heads, elbows, and eyeballs as they sat up.

"Did we just get pummeled by a spring-loaded wall?" asked Ellen.

"No," said Edgar. "We just got pummeled by a spring-loaded wall hiding *a secret tunnel*."

It was true. The brick wall was now flush against the ceiling, revealing the densely packed dirt beyond—packed except for a narrow, crude tunnel exuding the familiar scents of the sewers.

The twins, mouths agape, examined the hole. Just inside the mouth, they found a badly bent spoon.

"A spoon?" breathed Edgar. "Somebody dug a tunnel into our house with a *spoon*? That's determination."

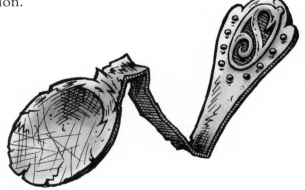

"That's *madness*," said Ellen.

Pet shined a flashlight into the tunnel, illuminating the slimy stones and murky waters of the sewer tunnels.

"How did this happen?" asked Edgar. "How did someone dig a tunnel *straight into our house* without us knowing about it?"

"I'll tell you how," said Ellen. "We've been so preoccupied with headlining festivals and teaching mischief classes that we forgot to protect our own home. Like amateurs!"

Pet swirled a tendril in the dusty ground, tracing out its peculiar form of writing.

*"Perhaps your lessons were too good, it's true,"* Edgar translated. *"You've taught the townsfolk how to think*

*like you*. Pet's right. This does have the hallmark of something we'd do."

"Yeah, back when we weren't leading parades, but instead lurking in the shadows behind them," said Ellen.

"Controlling attack robots!"

"And lobbing stink bombs!"

"And getting even," said Ellen, examining the spoon more closely. "Look."

The handle of the spoon had been caked with sweat-drenched dirt, obscuring some of its detail. Ellen scratched some of it away, revealing an initial engraved into the elaborately carved handle: a flamboyant *S*.

"*S*? You've got to be kidding," said Edgar. "That means—"

"Stephanie Knightleigh," growled Ellen. "The lavender menace returns."

"Then let's show her how happy we are to see her."

With Pet bounding behind, the twins dove headlong into the tunnel with a hearty song in their throats:

> *Perhaps our brains were overrested;*
> *Now we know that we've been tested.*
> *Enough! we cry, we won't be bested*

*By a Knightleigh heist.*
*Ah! Smell that stinky sewer slime!*
*Yes, revel in the goop and grime!*
*But it will truly be sublime*
*When Stephie's plans are iced.*

## 8. Debate and Switch

The spoon-dug tunnel spilled onto the broad stone boulevards of the Nod's Limbs sewer system—familiar territory, indeed, for the twins, even if it had been some time since they had properly skulked these byways.

"Where has Stephanie been since her family got run out of town?" asked Edgar.

"I always assumed in some dark room, curled up and crying in shame," said Ellen. "But maybe that got old after a while."

The trail of footsteps led past the magnificent gargoyles presiding at each tunnel intersection, and these stately monsters (all named by the twins) gazed down on them now as they traveled: regal Hammurabi, mopey Chuzzlewit, preposterous Bugsy. When they reached ax-wielding Maude, the trail led up a flight of metal rungs on the sewer wall, to a man-hole cover above.

"Looks like she surfaced," said Edgar. "Maybe she's hiding at her old house."

"Knightleigh Manor would be a terrible place to hide," Ellen pointed out. "They're turning it into a pigeon sanctuary."

"Only one way to find out," said Edgar.

Pet hopped up the rungs, leading the way, and it and the twins popped up in the middle of Founder's Park. Behind them, Nod's golden statue sat peacefully, its newly attached arms and legs gleaming in the sun.

But the rest of the park was not so peaceful. Just ahead of the twins, a large crowd gathered around a stage, clapping and cheering and whooping and hollering. Bob the interim mayor stepped up to the microphone.

"Nod's Limbsians! Thanks for joining us on this historic day—the first ever Nod's Limbs mayoral debate! Please welcome our two candidates, construction-company chairperson Eugenia Smithy, and acclaimed action-movie star Blake Glide!"

"*Those* are the two best candidates they can muster?" said Edgar. "It almost makes me nostalgic for a Knightleigh in office."

The twins and Pet followed the crowd, trying to keep out of sight. They could hear Eugenia's voice boom out across the park.

". . . and I will officially be running on a no-prank platform! Why, just today someone put Dodie Watkins's chicken coop on wheels and rolled it right away. Prank, you say? I'd say the chickens call it 'theft.' What's next? Put the clock tower on wheels and roll it away? What about each of your homes?"

The crowd murmured in discontent.

"If someone took the clock tower, how would we tell time?"

"If someone took my house, what would I vac-uum?"

"What a loudmouth," muttered Ellen. "This town will never fall for Eugenia's trash talk. They love *us* too much."

"Don't worry," said Edgar. "I have all kinds of nefarious schemes in store for Election Day. Eugenia will get her due. . . . Assuming we wrap up this break-in business in time, of course. . . ."

"Look," said Ellen. "The boot prints stop right at the edge of the stage. It's like she just disappeared."

"Or finally realized she was tracking sewer sludge and wiped her feet," replied Edgar. The twins continued to sneak about while the debate continued.

"Excuse me, Ms. Smithy, but what about Prank You Very Much Day, and the Very Pranky Pranksters' Parade, and Pranksgiving?" Blake Glide retorted onstage. "We'd lose half our festivals under your regime. Are you against festivals, *too*, Eugenia?"

The twins could hear an audible gasp from the townspeople.

"Of course not! That's not what I said—"

"I don't think the good people of Nod's Limbs are concerned about mischief," said Blake Glide. "I think they're concerned about when they can wear their tuxedos and evening gowns to another red-carpet movie premiere. Well, if *I'm* mayor, we'll have movie premieres every weekend!"

"Pet, can you crawl under the stage to see if Stephanie's left any clues?" asked Ellen. Pet nodded and hurried under the platform. But it was not gone more than a minute before it shot out again, covered in sawdust. It hopped up and down, then pointed frantically to the stage.

"What? What is it?" asked Edgar.

Just then, a terrible cracking sound came from the stage. Bob, Blake Glide, Eugenia Smithy, and everyone in the crowd heard it too. Before anyone could

respond, the stage broke apart in a cacophony of snapping wood and screaming mayoral candidates.

The twins and Pet jumped away, shocked. Bob was the first to emerge from the pile of debris, rubbing his bruised forehead.

"Well, that was a doozy," he said.

Blake Glide shoved a board off his head. "What kind of shoddy construction is this? I could have been killed! Or worse, scarred!"

Eugenia clawed her way out of the rubble. "My

construction company erected this stage this morning, and I can assure you, it was of the highest quality."

"Ah! Ah! You heard her! She's admitted to it! She's tried to assassinate me!" cried Blake Glide.

"I was up here too, you nitwit," said Eugenia. "I—"

"I'M BLEEDING!" screamed the action star. He held up his thumb, which did, indeed, have a tiny line of red dripping down it.

"That's not blood," said Eugenia. "It's red paint. I've got some on me too." She examined her hands, covered in sticky red. "And . . . gray." She started flinging the broken pieces of wood, clearing away a small patch of ground. Meanwhile handywoman Jill Geronimo came forward and began inspecting the stage's broken support beams.

"Sawed clean through," she marveled. "It's a wonder it didn't collapse straightaway. Someone did this on purpose!"

Eugenia threw up her hands triumphantly.

"Citizens! This is what I'm talking about! This was nothing more than an ill-conceived prank, and someone could have been seriously injured. See here, the perpetrators are none other than Edgar and Ellen!"

"Hey, you can't blame us for this!" said Edgar.

The crowd turned toward the twins, noticing them for the first time. Ellen elbowed her brother in the gut.

"Maybe you shouldn't have left a calling card, then," said Eugenia. "Look."

Edgar, Ellen, Pet, and the rest of the townspeople crowded around Eugenia, where she'd cleared away enough wreckage to reveal a note scrawled onto the ground in red and gray paint:

PRANK YOU VERY MUCH!

——EDGAR & ELLEN

"Uh-oh," said Edgar, as murmurs billowed up from the crowd:

"So this was a prank, then? I guess it wasn't 'funny ha, ha.' More like 'funny ouch.' Is that a kind of funny?"

"I don't know. I suppose so. Although it does seem like a prank with a high risk for splinters, and those are definitely not funny."

"No, not funny at all. Plus this lovely stage was destroyed. Perhaps this was going too far?"

"Of course it was," said Eugenia. "These pranks are poison for our town. They're dangerous. This isn't even a prank. It's *attempted murder*!"

"Hogwash," said Edgar. "Besides, we were framed!"

"But we know who did it," said Ellen. "Stephanie Knightleigh."

The townspeople considered this, and some of them clucked or tsked with skepticism:

"Seems unlikely."

"A disgraced Knightleigh would never dare come back."

"She was mean, but rather delicate."

Marvin Matterhorn grabbed Pet and held it up for all to see.

"See here. It's that guinea pig that's always following them around. It's covered with sawdust— something one might be covered in if one has been sawing stage support beams."

"Lies!" cried the twins in unison.

"Well, okay, Pet *is* covered in sawdust . . . ," began Ellen.

"I think it's time for Operation: Flee the People," Edgar whispered to Ellen. He pulled a bulky bundle from his satchel, then pressed a button. The package whirred and unfolded into a compact jet pack.

"You children won't escape justice once I'm mayor," said Eugenia.

Edgar slipped the jet pack over his shoulders and hit the launch button. Hot flames shot out from the back, and he began to rise off the ground. Ellen clung to his footies as Edgar took a fishing rod from his satchel, and then cast a line toward the dusty "guinea pig" in Marvin Matterhorn's hand. With a *twaaang*, Pet sprung free and was reeled to safety in the skies. The townspeople could only talk fretfully with one another, shading their eyes to follow the twins' aerial escape.

## 9. A Hat Is Thrown into the Ring

The crowd dispersed, but Mr. Hirschfeld remained, staring at the collapsed stage.

"I don't know . . . I just don't know about our candidates . . . ," he muttered to himself. "Not the best for this town. Not the best we can do . . ."

He wandered out of the park with his hands clasped behind his back, clucking to himself as he pondered the town's dilemma.

"A celebrity politician? Unheard of. Very

unseemly," he said. "Versus an antiprank platform? Now *that* just seems unfair to our beloved town founder. I wonder what he thinks about all this. . . . Wait! That's it!"

Ernest Hirschfeld turned on his heels, and then strode with purpose and conviction toward the southern end of town. When he reached the gate surrounding the twins' house, he pressed the intercom button.

*Bum ba, ba, baaa bum!* "The Flight of the Valkyries," echoed throughout the mansion, rousing Nod from an agreeable nap.

"Counfound that racket! Twins! What are you up to?"

*Bum ba, ba, baaa bum!*

This jarred Nod so badly, he knocked over the quills and pot of ink next to the divan where he had been napping.

"Hang it all," Nod grumbled, making his way to the intercom.

"Who is it?" he spoke gruffly into the speaker.

"Mr. Nod, my name is Ernest Hirschfeld, and I need to speak with you about an important mat—"

"You're not one of those performing guppie salesmen, are you? Because we already have one pet in the house, and it's strange enough!"

Mr. Hirschfeld was rather taken aback by the question.

"Guppies? No, sir. I come on an entirely different matter."

"Well, speak your bit, then. I may be living longer, but I'm not getting *younger*, you know."

"Of course, sir. I have come to inform you of the dire straits this town finds itself in. You may know, sir, of the two candidates vying for our mayorship? One Eugenia Smithy and one Blake Glide. And, I am sorry to say, neither seems fit for the job."

"What's that got to do with me?" Nod demanded.

"Sir, I believe there is but one man who could lead this town. A man of honor, of courage, of experience. A man who dedicated his life to Nod's Limbs. You, sir, are the man of whom I speak."

"I didn't dedicate anything to Nod's *Limbs*, you fool. When I went underground, it was still Nod's *Lands*. Missing limbs, my foot. Who names their town after a deformed statue?"

"Yes, who indeed, sir? Nod's Limbs, that's who!" said Mr. Hirschfeld. "That's the sort of spirit we need here, sir, and that's why I'd like to nominate you for mayor. Who better to lead this town than its founder?"

"Mayor! Are you as mad as a haberdasher?"

"Ah . . . do you mean *hatter*, sir?"

"Who knows? Why would I want to be mayor? Was this your bird-brained idea, Fishfield?" the speaker crackled.

"Uh, Hirschfeld," said Mr. Hirschfeld. "And yes, it was my brains, sir, not a bird's."

"Well, I don't want to!" Nod shouted into the speaker, so loudly it disrupted a pigeon sitting on the gates below.

"Your modesty is admirable," said Mr. Hirschfeld. "Nod's Limbsians love a modest leader."

"Go away!" Nod yelled.

"Yes, sir, we're going to go all the way with this!" said Mr. Hirschfeld. "I'll get started on the campaign right now. You won't be sorry, Mr. Nod!"

"I'm sorry you brought your poor excuse for a melon head to my gates!" Nod fumed. "I don't want to be mayor, you numbskull! I don't like people! I don't like leading people! I don't even like talking to people through gate security systems! So you can take your campaign and—"

But Mr. Hirschfeld had already left the mansion entrance and heard none of Nod's tirade or protestations. He walked briskly back to town, thinking of all the wonderful campaign slogans and signs he would make to rally the people behind their fearless town founder.

## 10. We Interrupt This Program

Edgar steered the jet pack back toward the mansion, where the twins and Pet landed on the cupola, then entered the roof-top elevator. The eleventh-floor penthouse suite had been trans-formed into a retreat for Pet, including a cushy mound of pil-lows for lounging; an old, leather, wingback chair (one of the few items salvaged from the collapse of the twins' old house); and a tele-vision. Pet noticed the time on the grandfather clock and flew to the television, flicking it on with a tendril. Then it reclined back on the wingback chair.

"We're in the middle of a domestic crisis, and still Pet has to catch *Around the World With Professor Paul*," muttered Edgar. "Pointless nature show."

*"The Barkudia skink lizard lives a precarious life in the swamps of the Magaloon Delta,"* whispered Professor Paul from the TV. *"Watch as it hops from lily pad to lily pad, every corpuscle in its cold-blooded body poised for an attack from unseen dangers nearby."*

Pet watched in horror as two eyes broke the swampy surface. A pair of cold pupils fixed on the skink.

"Actually, this is sort of interesting," said Ellen.

*"Leap, little lizard! Leap!"* cried Professor Paul, but the skink failed to obey. The eyes of the predator inched closer, and Pet covered its eye.

*"DEATH AT YOUR LILY PAD, SWEET SKINK!"*

Behind the little lizard, a vicious maw with three rows of needlelike teeth, opened wide.

*"Great lizard in the sky! Too late! It's too—"*

*Bzzzipp!*

"Well, hi, there!" said a peppy female voice. "Sorry!"

Pet peeked out from behind its tendril. Natalie Nickerson, the regionally famous news reporter, stood onscreen wearing a yellow hard hat and clutching a microphone in a rubber-gloved hand. She stood in front of a dirt-caked glass door.

"We sincerely apologize for interrupting our regularly scheduled program to bring you this Nod's Limbs Action Eyewitness News special report. I'm reporting to you *live* from our neighboring town to the west, Smelterburg." The newswoman pushed the filthy door open and beckoned the camera to follow. "And what you are about to see may shock you."

The twins were intrigued. Nobody from Nod's Limbs ever ventured beyond the last covered bridge of their town. Smelterburg, under the rule of industrial legend Mayor Blodgett, was believed to be unfit for any respectable Nod's Limbsian.

Natalie Nickerson stopped at a second door; one marked EMPLOYEES ONLY. "I'm in the back hallway of the city's most popular eatery, the Smelterburger." She pressed her other gloved hand against the swinging door. "It might be wise to send the children from the room now," she warned.

The door opened into the restaurant's kitchen, where a large, sweaty figure in a dirty apron and hairnet wielded a greasy spatula over a sizzling grill.

"No way." Edgar stepped up to the screen. "No. Way."

"Yes, my fellow Nod's Limbsians," said Natalie Nickerson. "It's true. The man behind the burger buns is none other than . . ."

## 11. Flipping Out

"Knightleigh!" shouted a burly, bald man with tattoos on both biceps. He tossed a half-eaten plate, like a discus, down the long metal counter. "Ain't no pickle on this deluxe! Ain't got no pickle, ain't no deluxe! Fix it!"

"A pickle makes a nickel, sir!" The former Nod's Limbs mayor smiled nervously. "Sorry, Mr. Crubbs! One pickle coming up!"

Natalie Nickerson slinked toward the cooking line where the ex-mayor flipped, dipped, and sweated.

"I'm going to get a closer look," she whispered loudly above the clinking of glasses and the barking of food orders.

The former mayor's hands darted in all directions, spinning the ticket wheel, flipping three burgers, tossing the French-fry basket, then flipping three more burgers. He spun with the grace of a ballroom dancer as he lifted the deep fryer from a pool of boiling oil, then whirled again to slide two burgers onto a bun bottom, adding cheese, onions, and a tomato slice with a blink of an eye, before slapping on the bun top.

The display was more intense than a skink lizard's death scene.

As ex-Mayor Knightleigh turned back to grab a fresh clump of ground beef, he froze and sniffed the air.

"What is that smell?" he said to himself. "Onions? Grease?" Sniff, sniff. "No, no." He rolled his head in a slow circle, sniffing again. "I smell . . ." He shot a glance right into the television screen. "A camera!" Knightleigh leaned in and smiled. "I knew I smelled the tools of publicity! Hello out there, anonymous viewers!"

"Uh, greetings, uh, Mister, um, ex-Mayor Knightleigh," stuttered the reporter, stepping out from behind the pickle barrel.

"Goodness!" The former mayor clutched the reporter in a big, sweaty bear hug. "Miss Nickerson! How wonderful to see you!"

The reporter was speechless. And damp.

"I've wanted to reconnect with my longtime constituents and show off my new job!" The politician set Natalie Nickerson down and removed his hairnet. "For tasty meals, look no further—come on down to Smelterburger!" he sang.

"Knightleigh!" Mr. Crubbs barked off-camera. "Get your tail in gear! We got the lunch rush comin' in!"

"Right away, sir!" Knightleigh whispered to Natalie Nickerson, "If I play my cards right, I could make *shift manager* by the end of the month!"

He returned to his burger flipping, and Natalie Nickerson turned back to the camera.

"Well, there you have it, folks. Our once-esteemed mayor, nearly shift manager. But what has happened to the rest of the mayoral family?"

"Yes, what?" said Edgar.

The camera cut to a department-store cosmetics counter, where Judith Stainsworth-Knightleigh stood in a white lab coat, dusting a portly woman's face with powder.

As the camera came closer and closer to the unsuspecting saleswoman, Natalie Nickerson's narration continued: "We warn you about the footage we're about to show you. Such scenes of humiliation might be unsettling to more sensitive viewers."

On the tape, Judith Stainsworth-Knightleigh finally noticed the camera, and she leaped to cover it with her hand.

"Get that camera out of my face," she said haughtily. "I didn't lead this company in lipstick sales three months running by gabbing to the press!"

"And, of course," continued Natalie Nickerson's voice-over, "Miss Stephanie Knightleigh is also learning to make her way in the world."

"Yeah, by turning to a life of crime," Ellen seethed.

"Here's the scene earlier this month at the Smelterburg wharf," said Natalie Nickerson. The camera showed a decrepit-looking boating dock, where a handful of people were boarding an even more decrepit-looking boat. Waiting to get on the gangplank was Stephanie Knightleigh, although at first, it was hard to recognize her. She wore a drab, uncomfortable-looking gray school uniform and sensible brown shoes. Her hair had lost its bounce, and her eyes were red and puffy.

"Can you *believe* they're shipping me off," she screamed, "to a boarding school in some rainy country I've never heard of? They sold my entire purple

wardrobe to pay for it. All of my ball gowns, tiaras, even the poodle skirts—*gone*." The girl sobbed. "I was going to be mayor! Mayor, I tell you—"

The camera cut back to Natalie Nickerson at the restaurant. The reporter shook her head. "Trying, indeed, for one so young. And yet is this a fitting price to pay for bamboozling an entire town, and burying three children and an old man alive? We at Action Eyewitness News leave you to judge. The youngest Knightleigh, at least, is weathering the change slightly better. . . ."

A waving hand burst into view from somewhere below the camera. "Hello, television friends," squeaked a voice, and the camera tilted down to show the rest of the hand's body: It belonged to a young boy in a grass-stained shirt and patched trousers. He looked as cheerful as a birthday balloon.

"Miles!" exclaimed the twins.

"Yes, ladies and gentlemen," said the reporter, "I'm here with Miles Knightleigh, who agreed to join me on-camera—"

"And show you where my dad works," said Miles. "Don't forget you owe me an ice-cream cone!"

"Ah, yes, of course," said the reporter, blushing. "Miles, what have you been up to since your family's devastating fall from power?"

"Been busy," he said. "Climbing trees, skinning knees, stomping puddles—the usual stuff. For a little bit I lived with some neat-o friends in Nod's Limbs, helping them redecorate their house. But then my family came back to get me—"

"Yeah, and I had to finish blowtorching the brass railings by myself," retorted Ellen, but she didn't sound that angry with the boy who helped the twins thwart the Knightleighs one final time.

"Well, you look like you're as cheerful as ever,

Miles," said Natalie Nickerson. "You must really like Smelterburg!"

"Nopers," he said. "I think it's stinky. But I'm happy, because I'm going to summer camp today and getting away from my family. They nearly left me and my friends buried underground. Did you tell everybody that? Because that's what they did. That, and they stole stuff. They're stealers."

The reporter looked surprised.

"Never let them forget it, Miles," said Edgar.

"There you have it, Nod's Limbs," finished the reporter. "Time marches on, even for the Knightleigh family. And now back to your regularly scheduled program."

Professor Paul flashed back onto the TV. The twins looked at each other. Ellen burst out laughing.

"Oh. Oh, this is too good," she roared. "Did you see Stephanie? Like she's been sleeping on doormats for a month! Ha, ha, ha, ha!"

"Uh, Ellen, I hate to burst your bubble, but that looked very much like an ocean that Stephanie was about to cross," said Edgar.

"So?" asked Ellen, wiping tears from her eyes.

"Well, if she's on another continent, she couldn't

very well have broken into our house and stolen anything."

Pet pulled the spoon from Edgar's satchel and made a scooping motion with it.

"Oh right, not to mention digging a tunnel with a spoon," said Edgar.

"But the *S*!" exclaimed Ellen, now entirely serious. "It's an ornate silver spoon with an *S* on it! Who else could it be? Who else has her picture under 'nemesis' in the dictionary? It *has* to be Stephanie."

"I don't know what to tell you. The evidence says it isn't."

Ellen growled like a wildebeest.

"But that means we're back to the question: Who has a grudge against us whose name starts with an *S*?" Edgar continued.

"And knows the sewers pretty well," added Ellen.

The twins thought for a moment.

"I can only think of one person who fits that description," said Ellen.

Edgar nodded. "Eugenia *Smithy*."

## 12. So Dark the Con of Mason

Within the hour, the twins and Pet were standing in an old haunt they hadn't visited in a long time. Eugenia Smithy, now a mayoral candidate, had at one point assumed a hidden identity as the Mason, a secret only the twins knew. Back then, she had turned a maintenance room in the sewers into her own underground lair from which she would plot her schemes. As the head of Smithy & Sons & Daughter Construction, she knew the sewers like the back of her hand. If Eugenia Smithy was behind the thefts, this seemed the most logical place where she'd stash incriminating evidence.

But the room was empty.

True, the bookshelves, chairs, and rugs were still right where they'd always been, and the stately oil paintings still hung, albeit slightly crookedly. Cobwebs and grit coated the leather chair in the center. The cast-iron furnace held only long-cooled clumps of ash. Edgar had long since relieved this chamber of its collection of antique tools, but the other trappings had remained largely untouched—except for a fresh scroll of paper unfurled on a side table, a precisely drawn blueprint of the sewers. Scrawled over its crisp white lines were handwritten markings. These scribbles included measurements between certain surface landmarks, calculations of distance, estimations about metric tons of dirt, and one sinewy tunnel between a sewer line and a sketched-in box labeled TOWER SUBBASEMENT (ESTIMATED LOCATION). In the corner of this blueprint, stamped and official, was the logo of Smithy & Sons & Daughter Construction.

"Bingo," said Edgar.

"Look at this," said Ellen, pulling open a drawer. Inside was an open velvet case filled with a row of spoons. On one end, a dusty outline suggested that one had recently been taken. Ellen picked one up and ran her finger over the S engraved on the handle.

"S for 'smoking gun,'" she said.

"Or 'stupid to leave all incriminating evidence lying around,'" said Edgar. "So do we wait here for her to come back?"

Ellen's gaze fell upon the sewer blueprints, and her eyes lit up.

"No," she said. "We pay her a visit right now."

"At the Smithy yards?"

"No, I know where she's spending all her time." Ellen stabbed the map with her finger. "It's a lovely day to tour the Waxworks, don't you think?"

Pointing the way with the crooked spoon, the twins marched into the sewer, singing at the top of their lungs:

> *Long this fiend has held a grudge—*
> *Our best-laid plans she sought to fudge.*
> *But lo! Our feet refuse to budge;*
> *We shall yet win the day!*
> *She dared intrude into our dwelling*
> *(Though it's our fault for poor repelling)*
> *But now betrayed by spoonly spelling—*
> *Eugenia's going to pay!*

## 13. Get Your Wax Straight

Scaffolding and cranes surrounded the old Wax-works, where Nod had begun his candle empire two centuries ago. As Edgar and Ellen crept closer to the factory, they could see men in hard hats carrying fresh planks of wood, bags of cement, and blocks of beeswax. One thick fellow in a cherry picker marked SMITHY & SONS & DAUGHTER was hanging a sign on a tall pole that read: TOUR THE NEW OLD WAXWORKS! OPENING THIS FALL.

"Lots of bodies here," said Edgar. "It will be hard to take Eugenia by surprise."

"So we lie in wait until the perfect moment to strike," said Ellen. "And I know just where we can hide. Follow me."

Edgar and Ellen slipped, slithered, and snuck their way around piles of bricks and stacks of pipes. As they drew closer to the Waxworks door, they deftly dodged the attention of the construction workers and crouched behind a pair of sawhorses (which, although narrow as all sawhorses are, provided unusually good cover for the trim twins). They were nearly spotted by Steve, the mustachioed foreman, but at the last moment the snack truck pulled onto the job site, tooting its horn, and the whole crew took a midmorning break for coffee and churros. The twins slipped inside and ran for an office marked AUGUSTUS NOD: PROPRIETOR.

"What makes you think Eugenia will come here?" asked Edgar.

Ellen jerked a thumb toward a small note card tacked on the door that read. EUGENIA SMITHY: SITE BOSS. DO NOT DISTURB IF DOOR IS CLOSED!

"She's using this as her headquarters while she manages the Waxworks job," said Ellen. "When she's not on the campaign trail, she'll be here. Plotting something rotten, no doubt."

They rifled through the desk, which was full of Waxworks schematics and official Smithy & Sons & Daughter documents about lumber costs and concrete deliveries. They found no sign of Nod's letters, but when Edgar pulled out the bottom drawer of the desk, he discovered some familiar objects: a dark green hooded cloak and a pair of night-vision goggles.

"These don't look like standard construction gear, Sister."

"For carpenters, no." Ellen chuckled. "But they're the perfect thing for the Mason."

"So where's this hiding spot?" asked Edgar.

Ellen approached the portrait of Nod that hung behind the desk. The picture swung outward on hinges, revealing a secret compartment within, as the twins once discovered when Blake Glide had fallen through it headfirst. The gaping hole in the canvas remained, since the town-wide debate still raged over whether it should be repaired or left as testimony to the moment that had begun the treasure hunt that had changed the town so completely.

"This is it?" asked Edgar.

"It's concealed and out of the way," said Ellen.

"Eugenia must be spending a lot of time here. What could be better?"

The twins slipped into the nook behind the portrait. Through the hole, they could see out the office door and onto the vast factory floor, where full-bellied workers were returning to their posts. Their stakeout had begun.

"Do you have any churros in that satchel, Edgar?"

"No."

"Oh. It's going to be a long day, then."

## 14. Eugenia's Private Conference

The day wore on. Edgar and Ellen watched construction crewmen and -women come and go, sanding floors and running electrical wire. A few times they spied Pet dashing about the factory, playing pranks on the workers. The twins had to bite their tongues to keep from laughing when Steve's pants got caught mysteriously in a hydraulic dipping apparatus and he took a dunk in a vat of fresh wax.

"Good one, Pet," they snickered.

By early afternoon, their patience paid off: Eugenia stormed into the factory. After she chewed out Steve for wearing taped-together churro wrappers for pants, she pulled him into Nod's office.

"The campaign's going to start heating up, Steve," she said. "I need to know I can rely on you to run things at the Waxworks, so I can hit the trail harder."

"Sure thing, Ms. Smithy," said Steve. "I wouldn't worry so much. We believe in you."

"Thanks. But that blowhard Glide is out there, dumbing down the debate with his empty-headed glitz and glamour. Plus there's a nuisance on the horizon. Nod's little protégés are making trouble. They're really going to distract me from my mission."

"Aw, those little tykes. They make me chuckle."

"Doggone it, Steve! They're not amusing; they're civic nuisances! I'm going to toss them into jail the day I take office."

"Gosh, Ms. Smithy, that'll be kind of hard," Steve continued. "I don't know if you noticed, but Nod's pretty popular right now. He's really gaining in the mayoral race—"

"He *what*? When did he start running?"

Steve winced. "Oh, uh, this morning. Didn't you hear? It was all over the radio. Mr. Hirschfeld is his campaign manager, and he says they're going all the way."

The twins exchanged puzzled looks in the dark behind the portrait. Eugenia, however, merely screamed.

"Gosh, don't let it bother you, Ms. Smithy. He's only second in the polls. He won't catch Blake Glide. Sounds like Mr. Glide's free-popcorn-at-the-movies platform is really catching on—"

"Only second . . . ? Oh, this tears it! Steve, I have some private work to do. Get back on the job and leave me alone for a while. Oh, and Steve?"

"Yes, Ms. Smithy?"

"Get some proper pants!"

After the door closed, Eugenia opened the desk drawer and withdrew the cloak and goggles. She dumped her Mason gear into a briefcase, then strode out. The twins followed.

They trailed Eugenia out of the factory and into the sewer culvert, taking care not to let their footies slap onto the cold stones.

"What was that nonsense about Nod running for mayor?" whispered Edgar.

"Some overeager reporter must have invented that cockamamie story," replied Ellen quietly. "No way is Nod running for mayor."

Up ahead, a cross-looking Pet held a small strand of hair in front of its eye, a sign the twins took to mean *"shhh,"* since Pet lacked both a finger and a mouth. It beckoned them forward.

"She's not heading toward her Mason headquarters," noted Ellen.

"Maybe she has a new lair," whispered Edgar. "That's why we didn't find Nod's stuff in the first one."

Finally, about twenty yards past Grungus the gargoyle, Eugenia stopped beside a wide iron pipe that ran from floor to ceiling. The twins and Pet peeked from behind Grungus's belly.

Eugenia pulled a wrench from her cloak and unbolted a coupling in the pipe. With a few quick turns and a firm rap with the wrench, the coupling came loose and slid down the pipe. The gap it revealed was hardly big enough for Eugenia to fit through—and, indeed, if Edgar and Ellen had not been experts in infiltrating narrow spaces, they wouldn't have believed how quickly their quarry slipped up the pipe and disappeared from view.

"We haven't infiltrated a building through its drain pipe yet today," Ellen said.

"Let's correct that, shall we?" said Edgar.

## 15. Pasta La Vista

Edgar cocked an eyebrow when he saw where the pipe led them: a drain in the floor of a cafeteria kitchen. He craned his head cautiously out of the hole.

Ellen nudged him from below. "Keep moving! It's cramped down here."

"Shh! I don't see Eugenia yet. . . ."

"Then it's the perfect time to move!" Ellen stretched Pet like a rubber band and aimed its eyeball at her brother's bottom. Pet winced. Ellen let the creature fly, and both her brother and the hairball shot out of the drain pipe like spitwads from a straw.

"That's better," said Ellen, pulling herself out. "The view was horrible down there."

"Stealth mode," Edgar whispered. "You're going to get us caught."

"The only thing I'm catching right now is a whiff of cafeteria spaghetti. Where are we?"

The kitchen was the sort of bland, charmless kind specific to school cafeterias and summer camps. In the glare of the fluorescent lights, they could see industrial-sized pots of spaghetti, cooling on a counter. The twins crept to a window that overlooked a vast hall of folding dining tables and chairs. A colorful crest on the wall answered Ellen's question:

GRAND LODGE OF THE ROYAL KERFUFFLE
ORDER OF THE PERSIMMON PAPYRUS
NOD'S LIMBS CHAPTER

The crest was adorned with a dozen flags of different nations and several unusual carvings such as a dog blowing a trumpet, an ostrich laying a golden egg, and an upside-down pyramid upon which a hieroglyphic-like pharaoh danced a jitterbug.

"Oh, it's a fraternal order," said Edgar.

"It certainly is infernal," said Ellen. "But *what* is it?"

"A *fraternal* order, Sister. It's an exclusive club for old men who like to get together and pretend they have secrets the rest of us don't know about," said Edgar. "Mostly I think it's an excuse to have parties without their wives and wear stupid hats."

"Eugenia broke into a hat club for old men?"

"Shh! Look!"

Edgar pointed to movement at the far side of the hall. A figure was coming in, struggling to carry something heavy.

"We've got her now," said Ellen.

The figure wasn't Eugenia, however, but an older gentleman wearing a fez topped with ostrich feathers, blinking holiday lights, and a sphinx head on a wobbly spring.

"See?" said Edgar. "Stupid hats."

"I think that goes beyond stupid," muttered Ellen.

The oddly hatted man was carrying what looked like a large rolled-up carpet, assisted by another man in another bizarre hat who carried the other end. They propped this bundle against the wall under the crest, then unfurled it. It was a long printed banner that read:

A ROYAL KERFUFFLE WELCOME

(OI! OI! OI! MOO!)

TO BLAKE GLIDE

CANDIDATE FOR MAYOR

AND INTERNATIONAL FILM STAR OF

SCREEN AND MOVING PICTURES!
($5 PER PLATE; $6 WITH MEATBALL)

"This is a campaign stop," said Ellen. "People are paying good money to listen to Movie Boy talk about himself. And all they're getting out of it is some mushy pasta in watery red sauce."

"So what does this have to do with Eugenia?"

*WHUMP!*

Things went dark for the twins. Or mostly dark. For though something was definitely obscuring their vision, they got pinhole-sized glimpses of what was going on. A woman in a hooded green cloak had thrown a deep colander pot over their heads, and was pushing them toward the drain in the floor. Before they could get their footing, the twins fell into the hole, jamming together in the narrow mouth and getting stuck at their waists. They struggled against each other, but their elbows and arms were wedged tight.

"You two gooses are *cooked*," said Eugenia, picking up a ladle and spatula.

"What are you going to do—spoon us to death?" said Ellen.

"Maybe I will," said Eugenia. "Maybe they'll

serve twin soup with a side of pigtail tonight."

Edgar squinted through a hole and saw a meatball float to the surface of one of the spaghetti pots. But it wasn't a meatball—it was an eyeball.

"Hey, Eugenia," he called, "time to get served!"

Eugenia glanced over her shoulder and saw the rogue meatball atop the pot. Pet pinwheeled out of the spaghetti, armed with dozens of meatballs in its hairy tentacles. It fired ball after ball of ground-beef fury at Eugenia's head. She shrieked under the torrent and fell back, tripping over the colander and landing headfirst into a barrel-sized mixing vat.

Pet toppled the pot it had been hiding in, spilling mushy pasta and watery red sauce across the floor. The steamy mixture pooled around the drain, making the twins just slippery enough to wriggle free.

"We know you broke into our house," said Edgar, as Eugenia emerged from the mixing vat, dazed. He unfurled the sewer map they had found in the Mason's lair. "Does this look familiar?"

"What are you talking about?" asked Eugenia. "I was never in your house."

"Right," said Ellen, brandishing the spoon. "Just like this isn't your heirloom utensil. You used this spoon to dig a tunnel straight into our basement."

"Then you stole Nod's papers," continued Edgar. "And you sabotaged that stage in Founder's Park, trying to convince people that pranking is dangerous. A dirty trick, blaming us for your own crime."

Eugenia stared Edgar in the eye. "Okay, smarty-pajamas. First, I had nothing to do with that stage. Second, if I wanted to break into your house, why would I need a map of my family's own sewer system? I know its ins and outs better than *you*. Plus that's not even my handwriting."

Edgar looked at the map. "It isn't?"

"And you, Little Miss Freakshow," Eugenia continued, pointing at Ellen. "I own a construction company. Why would I use a spoon to do my digging?"

"Well . . . ," began Ellen.

Eugenia nodded. "So maybe we both have the wrong culprit."

"Rubbish," said Ellen. "We've trailed you through the sewers and into this den of weirdness. Why all the sneakery, Eugenia?"

That's when Pet reached into an interior pocket of Eugenia's cloak and pulled out a small vial stoppered with a cork.

"No, don't!" yelped Eugenia.

Edgar examined the jet black bottle, then held up the label for Ellen to see:

COUGHING PEPPER
Add to Any Food for Guaranteed Misery!
Hours of Fun (for You)

"Okay, that's neat," said Ellen, "but what does that have to do with anything?"

"Don't you see, Sister? Eugenia was going to sabotage Blake Glide's special dinner with potential voters. Coughing pepper—that's wicked stuff!"

"He's an outsider!" Eugenia growled. "A phony! He has no right to come into this town and take this election from me. Me! A loyal Nod's Limbsian."

Edgar rubbed the back of his neck. "Maybe . . . maybe she's right."

"Are you kidding?" said Ellen. "You think she's *not* our thief?"

Through a crack under the kitchen door, they spied

moving shadows—someone was coming. Eugenia jumped to her feet and dove headlong into the drain. Before the twins could follow, the door to the kitchen burst open. The men in silly hats had found them.

"What's all this commotion?" said the one with the largest hat.

"Look, Supreme Hoo-ha, we've been infiltrated!" said the other.

"By Imhotep, we have!" bellowed the Supreme Hoo-ha. "Our imperial spaghetti dinner ruined, our secret bunker intruded upon by the uninitiated!"

The twins waved feebly.

"We're the pasta inspectors from the Department of Foodstuffs," said Ellen. "We're here on an anonymous tip about some overcooked noodles. . . ."

"No, you're not," retorted the Supreme Hoo-ha, his spring-mounted sphinx wobbling with his anger. "You're Edgar and Ellen, and you nearly got Blake Glide killed this morning. And now this?"

The other man nabbed the glass vial from Edgar's hand. "Look, Your Hoo-Highness, a vial of coughing pepper—just like that stuff we used on the Lodge of Billabongos last year—"

"Not in front of the outsiders, Subsergeant Binkley!" said the Supreme Hoo-ha. "Still, it looks like they were planning to spike our campaign dinner. Another example of a prank taken too far. Since this kitchen is a privileged chamber of the inner sanctum, I have the authority to administer justice as I see fit."

The Supreme Hoo-ha picked up the ladle and spatula.

The next sound the twins heard was the gentle *whoosh* of Pet jumping down the drain.

"Me next," said Edgar, leaping after it.

"Be seeing you," said Ellen, following suit.

As the twins emerged from the pipes back into the sewer, they mopped the sweat and spaghetti sauce off their brows.

"Great, now we have an entire fraternal order hounding us," said Edgar.

"No worries," said Ellen. "The only danger they pose is that I might die laughing if I see any more of their stupid hats."

## 16. The Trappings of Success

The twins followed faint traces of pasta sauce for a few yards, but the trail petered out quickly, leaving them clueless once again.

"You don't really think we're talking about a third sewer skulker, do you?" asked Ellen.

"She made some good points," said Edgar. "Besides, you saw it yourself: She's trying to ruin Glide's chances in the election. She has no motive to interfere with us right now."

"Then who?" asked Ellen. "Who else in Nod's Limbs would enter our house and steal from us? Who would destroy that stage and blame us?"

"Assuming it's the same person," said Edgar.

Ellen punched his arm. "What? I'm just saying it's possible there are two different villains at work," Edgar exclaimed.

"Bah. Edgar, you and your possibilities. If I don't smash something soon, I'm going to get very, very cranky."

"We know our intruder was using the Mason's hideout," said Edgar. "We should set up a trap nearby, and see what we catch."

"Trapping," said Ellen. "Good. That will keep my mind off smashing for a while."

They visited the town's new junkyard, which had been growing steadily since the events of the treasure hunt. For as boring as the twins found the citizens of Nod's Limbs to be, they had to admit, these same citizens had some interesting junk to discard, such as whole pallets of bobblehead dolls (a veritable treasure chest of oddly sized springs), a fifty-five-gallon drum of tapioca (the key ingredient in Edgar's special instant-glue formula), or the rusted tines of an industrial-strength garden tiller (perfect as the gears in a giant armored bicycle the twins planned to construct later in the summer).

Thanks to Nod, the twins could now afford most anything they wanted without having to scavenge parts. But old habits die hard, and the twins greatly preferred rooting about a grungy pile of discarded debris and inventing uses for each bit of bric-a-brac they could find. Besides, ordering from catalogs required a lot of waiting and patience, since the items one orders do not arrive instantaneously, as television cartoons sometimes insinuate.

Edgar found some air-conditioning ductwork, and Ellen a functional cotton-candy spinner. Pet nabbed a particularly nifty hydrogen-fuel cell—an unusually advanced scientific apparatus to find tossed aside in a small town dump, but the twins had long since learned never to question such mysteries. Combined with some elastic belts, a motion detector, and a dollop of tapioca glue, these meager items could combine to make a standard snag-and-bag trap.

Construction was elegantly simple. After all, if you had spent as many years building and disabling snag-and-bags for personal amusement, you, too, could have done it in your sleep. The twins hid their handiwork on a path near the Mason's lair, set the snare, and retreated behind a gargoyle to watch.

The meager daylight that trickled through grates turned pale and thin as night approached. Their stomachs rumbled, and Pet nourished the twins with Royal Kerfuffle meatballs it found stuck inside its mop. ("I thought they'd be warmer," Edgar noted.)

Not long after the full cloak of darkness had descended, the sound of running feet echoed down the sewer tunnels. The twins withdrew inside the widespread wings of Twisted Louie and waited.

Their quarry loped into view. He ran none too silently, and his heavy breathing—for they could tell from the sound it was a he—seemed almost louder than his footsteps. The stranger lit his way with a powerful flashlight, so the twins couldn't see his face. But then the stranger dropped the flashlight, and as it tumbled, its beam passed over the man's face for a fraction of a second.

But instead of illuminating a face, it revealed a paper bag.

The man was wearing a paper bag over his head, with two eye holes cut from it and an angry face scrawled on with a fat marker.

"What the heck?" Ellen whispered.

Edgar gestured for her to be silent, but the intruder had already halted, as if he'd heard them. The stranger clicked off his light and shuffled deeper into the darkness. The twins couldn't see where he had gone, but they knew it was now a standoff of purest silence. If they could stay still and silent long enough, they might convince this masked man that he hadn't heard anything at all, and he would continue into their trap. They tensed their muscles to stifle even the slightest rustle of pajama on stone.

After a few minutes, it appeared they had won. They heard footsteps again and saw the bouncing rays of a flashlight. They craned their necks to get another look at the mask, but the light beam was pointed at the ground.

The figure drew up right beneath them and

paused at the tunnel fork over which Twisted Louie presided; a turn to the right meant the snare . . . to the left, and their quarry would escape safely. But the mysterious figure seemed indecisive. Edgar held Ellen's elbow as she made to pounce.

"Darn sewers," the stranger muttered as he pulled a roll of paper from his pocket and spread it upon the sewer floor. The twins could plainly see the paper: a map of the sewers stamped with the Smithy & Sons & Daughter seal.

The man ran his fingers over the map, har-rumphed, shone his flashlight down each tunnel, then turned the map upside down.

"Darn maps," he muttered. Then he sighed and put away the map. "I can do this. Just like in *Ace Ranger*, where I played a forest ranger with incredible biceps and a keen sense of direction."

The figure took a deep breath and dashed to the left. Ellen was too stunned to pounce.

## 17. The Fickle Finger of Fame

"Seriously?" said Ellen. "Blake Glide?"

"Why would *he* break into our house?"

"Death wish?" suggested Ellen.

Edgar looked skeptical. They ran down the tunnel after Glide, taking no particular precautions to be quiet since the movie star himself was so loud.

Finally Glide stopped in a beam of light from a streetlight above. He climbed up to the manhole cover.

"Old Town?" whispered Edgar.

"I think," Ellen whispered back.

Perhaps the twins could be forgiven for not knowing precisely where they were, for Old Town was a section of Nod's Limbs they tended to avoid. Not for any reasons of fear, but simply because Old Town represented the oldest houses ever built in town, and among them their oldest residents. As prank locations go, old houses are merely uninteresting—that is to say, old houses *not built by Augustus Nod*. In the more typical old homes of Nod's Limbs, there were no pleasurable challenges for the modern mischief maker, such as slitherable air ducts, secret passageways, or hackable security systems. And to the experienced prankster, the older residents in such homes were not particularly satisfying targets; they might, for example, not hear the doorbell for an elaborately set-up pie-tossing device, or taste the difference between strawberry oatmeal and oatmeal with pickle curd. Thus, it was for lack of true creative brinksmanship that the twins mostly ignored this quiet neighborhood.

When they followed Blake Glide through the manhole cover, the first thing they noticed was not the quaint homes of Brisbane Street, but a wall of pea soup green and marigold stars (Nod's Limbs' town colors). It took them a moment to adjust their eyes and realize they weren't looking at some kind of bizarre cosmic event, but a battalion of yard signs. Every yard had at least one of these oversized billboards, and some yards bore two or three. Each sign sported a field of stars, and in the middle was just one word: EUGENIA!

"Criminy! This whole neighborhood's gone gaga for Eugenia," said Edgar.

"It makes sense," Ellen said. "She has the oldest family in town, and these are the oldest people in it."

"Why would Glide surface here? Unless . . ."

Edgar mused. "Hm. He's not up to a little anti-Eugenia campaigning is he?"

As if in response, the twins heard the familiar *shik-shik-shik* of someone shaking a can of spray paint.

*Pfffft. Pfffft.*

"The call of the graffiti artist," said Ellen.

They wound through the maze of election posters and found Blake Glide hunched over a sign spray painting these words beneath a star-spangled EUGENIA!: *"is mean."*

"That's it?" cried Ellen. "*That's* your big sabotage?"

Blake Glide startled so wildly, he fell into the sign and knocked it over. He stood up and tried to run, but he tripped over another yard sign. He was wearing sunglasses (which flew off his face) and a fuzzy hunter's hat (which fell down over his eyes). He whimpered for a moment before pulling the hat back up and peeking at his antagonists.

*"You?"* He sat up. "What are you two ghouls doing *here*?"

"Golly, Mr. Glide," said Ellen. "We're your biggest fans. We follow you *everywhere*."

"Aw, gosh, I didn't realize that," stammered

Blake Glide. "Well, if it's an autographed photo you'd like—Hey, wait a second, you're tricking again, aren't you?"

Edgar smacked his forehead. "This is such a pathetic attempt to gain votes, I almost feel sorry for you."

*"Almost,"* said Ellen, and she grabbed the actor by his ear, jerking him forward. "Did you dig a sewer tunnel with a spoon?"

"No!" squealed Blake Glide.

"Did you break into our house?"

"No!"

"Did you steal anything belonging to Augustus Nod?"

"No!"

"What's the capital of Iceland?"

"I have no idea! *I have no idea!*"

Ellen released his ear and he collapsed to the ground, sobbing. "He's telling the truth—at least about the Iceland bit, although the other stuff sounds believable too."

"So he's just another crooked poli—Hey, wait a second, where'd your paper-bag mask go?" said Edgar.

"What do you mean?" said the actor. "I haven't used a paper-bag mask since an experimental theater

piece in grad school. *Monologues of Meaninglessness.*
Did you see it?"

"So you weren't wearing a mask just now?"
demanded Ellen.

"Heck, no! An actor's skin is his most precious
commodity. A mask would only trap sebaceous
secretions that would cause my skin to break out—"

"It wouldn't fit over that ridiculous hat, anyway,"
said Edgar. "Sister, this means someone *else* was in
the sewers!"

"The man in the paper-bag mask!" Ellen gasped.
"He sensed we were there and hid. Then when
Hambone here stumbled past, we followed the
wrong guy!"

"The man in the paper-bag mask is our true
adversary!" said Edgar.

"'The man in the paper-bag mask,'" mused Blake
Glide. "That has a nice ring to it. Do you have an
agent for the script?"

Edgar snatched the spray-paint can from Blake
Glide's hand. "Give me this. You're an unworthy
prankster, Mr. Haircut. Now beat it; you're in our
way!"

Blake Glide looked relieved to be dismissed. But
before he could escape, Ellen grabbed him again.

"Please, no more ear! No more ear!" he wailed.

"Did you see anyone else down there tonight?" Ellen demanded. "Anyone or anything suspicious at all?"

Blake Glide looked anxious. "Well, I thought I saw *you*. Or one of you, at least. I couldn't imagine who else would be down in the sewer."

"Was he wearing a paper bag on his head?"

"M-maybe. I couldn't see. All I know is, I was walking down a tunnel, and I saw someone up ahead, climbing a ladder. I hid in the shadows—I got good at that when I played a rogue mercenary with a chip on his shoulder in *The Hunted and the Handsome*—"

"But what happened next?"

"Nothing! When I thought you had gone for good, I took off."

Edgar scratched his chin. "Can you remember anything about where you were? Was there a gargoyle nearby?"

"Oh sure! The ladder was right under this hideous rat-faced beast that was sinking its fangs into a wheel of cheese. It gave me the worst willies. . . ."

The twins looked at each other. "Old Cheesecake!"

Ellen shoved Blake Glide away. "Your usefulness is done. Begone!"

The actor sighed with relief and ran off without looking back.

"Sister, this can only mean one thing. Our target is holed up at—"

"What's all this razzmatazz out here?"

They jumped, not expecting to encounter anyone else in this sleepy neighborhood. When they turned, they saw not one, but a dozen good citizens approaching. And while some approached with canes, and others walked with stoops or slow gaits, they all had one thing in common: They each had silver hair that shone in the glow of the streetlights.

"Are you two lovely children volunteering to join the Old Town Action Committee's last-minute electioneering efforts?" asked a sweet-voiced older woman. "Does this old heart good to see a little civic up-and-at-'em coming from the next generation."

Edgar and Ellen saw members of this band pulling up the EUGENIA! signs and replacing them with bigger signs that read: OLD TOWN'S NOW FOR NOD! (SWITCHEROO AND TWENTY-THREE SKIDOO!)

"Nod? . . . Really . . . ?" stammered Ellen. "Uh, sure, we're here to help you, uh, get the word out."

"Wait a tick, Agnes," said another woman. "That there is a teenage type holding a can of spray paint. In my day, we called that sort of thing *suspicious*."

"Now, now, Mabel," said Agnes. "Just because these two cherubs are out past dark—*Oh my heavens to Betsy, there's graffiti on that sign!*"

Agnes pointed at Blake Glide's pathetic attempt to defame Eugenia.

"Look, lady," began Edgar, "we had nothing to do with that—"

"Aw, applesauce!" shrieked Agnes. "Harold! Fire up the golf cart and round up these two vandals."

"Why do we always get blamed for this stuff?" Ellen sighed. This time, it was she who dove headfirst down the open manhole, followed by Pet and Edgar. They heard Agnes call into the sewer after them:

"And she's *not* mean, she's just unelectable. Vote Nod!"

## 18. For Letter or Worse

Beneath Old Cheesecake's toothy maw, Edgar gave his sister a formal after-you gesture, and she charged up the ladder.

"I can't believe we didn't check the wax museum first," she said. "It's a brilliant place to hide."

Some time ago, the Nod's Limbs Museum of Wax stood as the crown jewel of the town's cultural offerings. Whereas most wax museums featured likenesses of celebrities and important historical figures, Nod's Limbs' institution featured replicas of the people just beyond its doors. Every citizen of the town had his or her own wax duplicate in the museum. For, after all, who wouldn't pay ten dollars (half price on Tuesdays) to see a monument to themselves carved in wax?

But the museum had suffered a devastating setback

when, during a visit by some out-of-town dignitaries, a certain pair of striped troublemakers turned the thermostat far, far too high, and the museum of wax statues became a museum of wax puddles.

Now, at long last, the museum was being restored, one citizen at a time, by historian, custodian, and wax enthusiast Ernest Hirschfeld. The grand opening was not for several more weeks, making the museum a perfect place to steal away from prying eyes.

Infiltrating the museum was as easy as jimmying open a trapdoor in the sewer ceiling, and this job was made even simpler by the trap door already lying open.

"Bag Man's about to get busted," whispered Ellen as she clambered up.

Each room of the museum showed significant improvement since the twins' last memorable visit. The Nod's Limbs Grammar School room had an almost completed Miss Croquet, grading math homework; and the post office display showed a cheery Mr. Crapple, shoving wax bills and shopping circulars into his wax mailbag. The Hall of Gardeners was coming along nicely, although Mr. Poshi currently lacked a head, as did his swan-shaped hedge.

"Where do we begin?" asked Edgar. "This place is huge."

Ellen tugged a pigtail in thought. Pet leaped atop her head and pointed out a sign on the wall:

SEE WHERE IT ALL BEGAN!
## AUGUSTUS NOD AND HIS LABORATORY
THIRD FLOOR

"That's not a bad hunch, Pet," she mused.

The third floor of the museum of wax had been given over entirely to a recreation of Nod's eighteenth century laboratory—or at least a wild guess at it. Mr. Hirschfeld had never seen the underground laboratory beneath the twins' old home, thus he had no concept of the intricate devices and bizarre contraptions that were the hallmarks of the truly mad inventor. The real lab was where Nod had learned to harness some of the balm's powers in his candles. This lab couldn't begin to come close. The tables and beakers upon them were real enough, and the Bunsen burners looked authentic, but, at best, the test tubes of colorful liquids were better suited to dying Easter eggs than taming the volatility of Nod's special wax.

The statue of Nod, however, was dead-on.

"They even got the knots in his beard," said Ellen. "Creepy."

"At least wax Nod smells better than the real thing," observed Edgar.

"Brother, look here!" Ellen called. She picked up a stack of envelopes from a counter and waved them triumphantly. "Our Bag Man has been doing some light reading."

"Nod's letters! We did it!"

"Well, we got the letters, but not the letter carrier." Ellen leaned out a window that had been left open. "Looks like he climbed down the trellis. Did he hear us coming?"

Edgar picked up a trash can and sorted through wads of paper. "Here's the rest of Nod's journals and papers. Bag Man clearly sorted through these and decided the letters from Benedict were the only ones worth reading."

"So Nod was right," said Ellen. "There really *is* a threat to the balm."

"Time to find out what Nod wouldn't tell us," said Edgar, as he unfolded a random letter and began reading:

Augustus, old boy,

Curious comments in your last letter. I realize
the balm kept you alive all these years. In our
travels, the circus has seen and heard of other
odd effects at balm springs in other towns. We
have our own myths and legends about what
each balm is capable of; but in the end, they
all lead to the same thing: madness, greed,
bloodlust, and other rudeness. Be cautious.

—B.

Edgar flipped through the rest of the stack. "A lot
of these things have formulas and scientific jargon on
them. Here's one that's almost in English." He read
aloud:

Augie,

O ominous day . . . The calculations in your
last letter seem valid. We've seen similar
effects at the Black Diamond Glacier, as well
as in the deserts of Zimmizoka. I am tempted

to take samples from each spring in order
to try out your formulas myself. . . . But, as
you know, fiddling with the balm is strictly
verboten to us Heimertzes. If you're right, then
our mission to protect the world's balm supply
is more important than ever.

Hoping you're as wrong as a foghorn at a
funeral,

Benedict

Ellen grabbed a slip of bright red paper. It was
curled, as if rolled up into a tube rather than folded
into an envelope. She read:

A—I know you have your own conjectures about
the whereabouts of other balm springs. We've
already discussed some of them, but I fear I've
said too much already. I'll reveal no more. You
cannot attempt this experiment you mention,
not even for the sake of science. It is a danger
beyond any we've imagined. The balm must
be left alone. Whatever you do, guard your

*research closely and your remaining balm samples even closer . . . for the sake of us all.*
—B.

"Nod wasn't joking when he said that 'fate of humanity in the balance' business," said Edgar. "I thought he was just being melodramatic."

Pet had been pacing on the floor, and it paused to give Edgar a worried look.

"We need to find Bag Man and put a stop to him," said Ellen.

"But we're fresh out of leads," said Edgar. "Our mystery man is long gone, and there's no sewer sludge to track this time. Now we have to wait for him to make the next move."

"*Wait?* I hate waiting." Ellen gripped the windowsill and stared into the darkness.

"Oh, he'll make another mistake soon enough," said Edgar. "And then he's ours. Come on, let's deliver these letters to Nod and get him off our backs."

# 19. Pollster's Paradise

The wide-bottomed chickadees announced the coming dawn, and trailing the rising sunlight, Clovis Bumnutter rode his bicycle on his morning paper route.

As he hauled past Nod's mansion, he tossed a copy of the *Nod's Limbs Gazette* with his patented Bumnutter Overhand Fling. Most days, this throw would have deposited another perfectly pitched paper onto the front steps of the mansion, but today the delivery was intercepted by Edgar's head as he walked up the driveway.

*Thump.*

Edgar tumbled as his sister erupted in laughter.

"Sorry, Mr. Edgar, I didn't see you!" called Clovis as he pedaled away.

Edgar sat up, rubbing his head.

"We should greet the dawn more often." Ellen snickered. "I had no idea it was so much fun."

"I'm too tired to care about my dignity. Let's just get these letters to Nod and—" Just then, his eyes fell on the morning's top headline, and he unfolded the paper. "Okay, this is getting out of hand."

TOWN FOUNDER NOD LEADS POLLS!
Surprise Last-Minute Entry Stuns;
Elates Many

"Time we had a word with the old man," said Ellen.

They took the elevator up to Nod's office. They expected to find it empty, but Nod was wide awake, tinkering with an intricate array of beakers and tubes that had sprung up since the twins had left. He muttered to himself as he adjusted flames and tightened hose fittings.

"Uh, Nod? Good news," said Ellen. "We found your letters."

At first the elderly gentleman did not hear them. "Haven't gone below thirty degrees yet, and the kinematic viscosity is still within ten centistokes— Oh! Children! Hello, what did you say? The letters?"

The twins and Pet fanned the papers out onto the floor, although it was already covered with more diagrams, formula-scribbled scraps of paper, and torn-out journal pages.

"Excelsior, my friends! Did you catch our perpetrator?"

"Not exactly, but we know who it is," said Edgar. "A man in a paper-bag mask."

"Oh, brilliant. That narrows it to any halfwit who carries his lunch to work." Nod scowled and tapped a tooth in deep thought. "Must work even faster now," he muttered. "Haven't tested the compression theory yet—"

"Nod, whatever you're doing with the balm, it can wait," said Edgar, waving the newspaper to him. "You need to explain this."

"This is a newspaper," said Nod, "wherein you will learn the winner of the kindergarten finger-painting contest, the average height of town grass, and other such rot. If you wish, you may use it to line birdcages."

But Edgar shoved the front page in front of Nod's face, so he couldn't miss the day's top story. "You send us out to stomp all day and night in the sewers with the fate of the world at stake, but you're up here kissing babies and glad-handing and inviting the Ladies Voting League over for tea?"

"What?" Nod nearly dropped the beaker he was holding. "What? How? I told that simpleton Hirschfeld I wanted nothing to do with this election! How can I be ahead in the polls?"

"Wait, you didn't know about this?" Ellen roared.

"Ha! Ha, ha, ha! That may be the best prank I've ever heard!"

Ellen grabbed the paper and skimmed the article.

"'"I like Mr. Nod's stance on the issues," said resident Francie Bean,'" she read aloud.

"What stance? I don't have a stance!" Nod protested. "Except 'wobbles a bit while walking.' *That's* my stance."

Ellen continued: "According to Dwight Strongbowe, 'Nod has a great outlook on lawn care. I appreciate that in a candidate.'"

"My only outlook on lawn care is that I don't care about lawns!" thundered Nod. "Twins, I can't have this distraction now. My work is critical. You have to sabotage my campaign."

Edgar and Ellen looked at each other and sighed.

"That seems to be the popular campaign strategy these days," said Edgar.

"Wait, Nod," said Ellen. "The man in the paper-bag mask! We've got to catch him!"

But Nod was already waving them off. "Yes, yes. You must and you will. I'm sure he hasn't gone far. But we have a more immediate problem. If I inexplicably become mayor, I will have a bee swarm of distractions just getting the busybodies at Town

Hall off my stoop. And I don't have time for that. I must devote all my time to these experiments!"

"Well, it would get us into town, where we can keep our eyes open for more suspicious activity," said Edgar. "Maybe we can kill two wide-bottomed chickadees with one stone."

Ellen scowled but remained quiet.

"That's the spirit!" said Nod. "Now, elections are tomorrow, which means you have to work fast. Do whatever you have to—stomp on any toes, pickle any fingers, whatever—just cost me that election."

"We'll do our best, Nod," said Edgar.

Nod raised his coffee mug.

"Here's to losing big!" he exclaimed.

The twins trotted off, singing a song under their breaths:

*While bigger threats still loom at large,*
*We're saddled with an extra charge.*
*But Nod commands; we say "Yes, Sarge!"*
*Now we've a fraud to plan.*
*The anti-odds we'll have to stack*
*To send this voting off the track,*
*And then it's time that we get back*
*To bagging our Bag Man.*

## 20. The Knightree Manor

The twins retired to the game room to plan their next step.

"Between Eugenia Smithy trying to sabotage Blake Glide, and Blake Glide trying to sabotage Eugenia Smithy, and Nod trying to sabotage himself, this has got to be the dirtiest election on record," said Ellen.

"And in our own little Nod's Limbs, no less," said Edgar. "And we're not even among the candidates! The times—how they change."

He unrolled some blueprints onto the billiards table.

"Bag Man will have to wait," he said. "Let Operation: Election Infection commence!"

"I don't know why you're all excited," said Ellen. "Clearly we just stuff the ballot boxes in either Eugenia's or Blake Glide's favor. I'd say Blake Glide. He seems to have the proper lack of credentials to run this town."

"It's not *what* we have to do, it's *how*," Edgar replied. "Remember those nefarious schemes I had for Election Day? Well, they're about to pay off."

"How so?"

"I placed a spy inside the operation. You know,

to report on how Bob is running the voting and where we can exploit it." Edgar rubbed his hands together. Ellen just shook her head.

"All right, I'll bite. Who is this spy of yours?"

"Sister! I have to protect the identity of an inside man!" Edgar said, pulling a pocket watch from his satchel. "But if all goes according to plan, we're rendezvousing in thirty minutes. Follow me!"

Edgar led Ellen and Pet out of the house and into the Black Tree Forest Preserve, which abutted their property. Edgar paused at the base of a mighty oak tree, deep in the woods, and cupped his hand to his mouth.

"Caw, caw! Caw, caw!" he called out to the trees.

"For crying out loud," muttered Ellen.

"Quiet, Sister. Wait for the all-clear signal."

*"Tweetereetereetereeterpatchoo!"* came a reply from the tree above, and a rope ladder dropped down in front of Ellen, nearly smacking her in the nose.

"Hey, watch it!" she said.

"Quiet!" barked Edgar. "Just climb."

Ellen put Pet on her shoulder and climbed up, with Edgar following behind. The rope ladder swung back and forth perilously, but the twins had the sure-footed climbing skills of squirrels. Even so, it seemed to take all day to climb. The air was warm and sticky, and Ellen felt beads of sweat across her forehead as they climbed. She looked upward and saw something strange above her, tucked among thick limbs and wide leaves. A massive structure was built around the trunk of the tree, like a gigantic tree fort. But it was *purple*.

"Just where are you taking us?" Ellen demanded.

"Don't worry, just keep going."

"I will not walk blindly into a purple tree house!" said Ellen.

"Then don't walk. Climb!" Edgar gave his sister a poke in the footie. "Don't be such a scaredy-cat."

That was all Ellen needed to hear. She sped up the ladder and through the trapdoor of the tree house. When Edgar popped his head through a moment later, Ellen shoved a fistful of Pet into his mouth.

"Ptooey!" he spat as Pet extracted itself. "That tastes terrible!"

"I could have told you that," said a voice behind them. "Never taste hair, no matter how tempting it looks!"

Ellen turned. Before her stood Miles Knightleigh.

## 21. Small-fry Spy

"Miles!" cried Ellen. "What are you doing here?"

"I'm an indoor man now!" piped Miles.

"*Inside* man, Miles," said Edgar. "Criminy, you're worse than Nod."

"Since when are you a spy for Edgar? I thought you were going to summer camp," said Ellen.

"I did!" said Miles. "And when the bus passed Nod's Limbs, I hopped out the back—according to plan, right, Edgar?"

"Edgar, you *planned* this?" said Ellen.

Edgar unleashed a torrent of guffaws.

"I'm brilliant!" He snorted. "We've been plotting his escape for *weeks*, and you never knew. I'm the master of misdirection—the duke of deception!"

"Yeah, yeah, and the baron of bigmouths," said Ellen. "Congratulations, Miles, on your escape from camp. It's not the worst thing in the world to have you back."

"Thanks, Ellen!" said Miles. "It's better than super to *be* back!"

For the first time, Ellen took in her surroundings. They were standing in a massive tree house, only it was unlike anything she had seen before. Most tree houses are built by dear old Dad, who promises the kids a place to play outside the regular, adult-infested home. They generally consist of a small floor and three to four walls, and, if you're lucky, a roof. They're stocked with sleeping bags, flashlights, action figures, secret things you don't want your parents or your nosy little brother to find, and sometimes a tin-can phone connected to the main house (used for asking Mom to bring out more snacks). By and large they are simple structures but ideal places to dawdle.

This tree house, on the other hand, was large enough to fit fourteen Mayor Knightleighs, six Gully Lugwoods, and a Principal Mulberry. And it wasn't just a floor with walls; it had actual *rooms*. There was a bedroom with bunk beds, a living room with a sofa and a chaise lounge, a mudroom to hang your coat and leave your boots, and a kitchen complete with pot-bellied stove (decorative only). And every-thing was purple.

"This was Stephie's last birthday present from Dad," said Miles. "But they couldn't fit her king-size canopy bed up here, so she gave it to me!"

"I can understand her displeasure," said Ellen.

"We have important business to attend to," reminded Edgar. "Miles, do you have anything to report?"

"Aye, aye, sir," said Miles, saluting Edgar. "Before Stephie left for boarding school I asked her a bunch of questions about how elections work in Nod's Limbs. Don't worry, Edgar—I was sneaky, just like your letter asked."

"Oh, right, Miles," said Ellen. "I'm *sure* she had no idea you were up to something."

"Have faith in my student," said Edgar. "He learned at the feet of a maestro."

"Here's what I learned," said Miles, unfurl-ing a map of town upon a table. He pointed to six red circles. "There are six voting places through-out town. Every person is given one ballot and a ballpoint pen, in order to check a box. At the end of the day, Mr. Bob"—and here Miles produced a telephoto snapshot of Bob the interim mayor—

"will collect all the votes from each polling place and load them in this truck." Miles pulled out a crude drawing of a mail truck with the word MALE written on the side. "Uh, it may not look exactly like this. Anyway, Mr. Bob will take the votes to a super-secret location, where he will guard them until the following morning, when he will count all the votes in front of everyone at Founder's Park."

"That's it?" asked Ellen.

"Yes," said Miles. "Devious, isn't it?"

"Gee, Edgar, I'm so glad you put your best man on this case," said Ellen.

"Where is the secret location, agent?" asked Edgar.

"Oh, I couldn't find that out," said Miles.

"What? Why not?" asked Edgar.

"It's super-secret!" said Miles.

Edgar sighed. "It's okay. We'll just have to work our magic before the close of the polls then."

"Yippee! Magic!" Miles squealed.

## 22. Swarm Embrace

Edgar, Pet, and Miles began rummaging through an old box of Stephanie's, marked DRESS-UP FUN! Edgar had crossed this out and written MASTER DISGUISES.

"We need to infiltrate the polling places, unde-tected," said Edgar, as he sorted costumes. "Miles, how do I look in this chef's hat?"

Ellen tossed up her hands. "For Pet's sake! Look, while you three play fashion show, I'm going to do something useful. Like hunt for Bag Man."

She was already climbing down the rope ladder before her brother could protest. She took the rungs two at a time, muttering to herself. "Ridiculous tree house. We should be on the streets. In the sewers. Under the tables. Anywhere we can catch the trail of the thief . . ."

Just then, the ladder began to shudder. In a mat-ter of seconds it shook so violently, it nearly hurtled Ellen into the air.

"Wh-what is th-this?" she said through gritted teeth.

Although the view straight down was obscured with branches and leaves, she could just make out a gray cloud swirling around the bottom of the ladder—

a swarm of insects. But the ladder seemed much shorter than it had a moment ago. In fact, its end was several feet above the ground. And still the bugs drew closer.

"Edgar!" cried Ellen. "What's g-going on?"

Her brother poked his head through the trapdoor.

"You're quitting the mission, that's what's going on!" he shouted. "I don't know why I—*What the heck is that?*"

"Bugs!" said Ellen. "A whole s-swarm of them. And I th-think they're—they're—"

"Oh, walnuts! They're *eating the ladder*!" cried Edgar. "Move it, Ellen! Climb! Climb!"

Ellen was halfway down the ladder, and the swarm of bugs was halfway to *her*. And every second the ladder grew shorter.

*"Criminy!"* Ellen climbed as fast as she could, but the vibrations in the rope grew stronger as the swarm drew closer. Her fingers could barely grasp each rung as the rope bucked wildly. She was nearly to the tree house, but the bugs were closing in. Eight rungs behind her. Seven rungs. Six.

"Hurry, Sister!"

Five rungs. Four.

Edgar gripped Ellen's hand and tried to pull her up. Her hands were sweaty and slick. She slipped from his grasp, but his other hand caught her wrist and he heaved.

Three rungs. Two rungs.

Ellen scrambled into the tree house, the swarm buzzing at her toes.

"My clippers, my clippers!" Edgar shouted, and Pet flung him a set of hedge trimmers from his satchel.

One rung.

*Snip, snip.* Edgar cut the ladder just in time, and the last rung—covered in crawling, biting black bugs—plunged back to the earth. Edgar and Ellen and Pet sprawled onto the platform, exhausted.

"They're worse than fire ants!" Edgar said. "Like flamethrower ants. Or big, erupting volcano ants . . ."

*"Yow!"* Ellen screamed. One of the insects had crawled into a hole in her footie pajamas, and was now taking large bites of her toe. She screamed again and stomped her foot. The little nasty shot out of the pajama hole.

Edgar plopped a glass jar over the pest, capturing it. "Got you!"

"Who's your hungry little friend, Ellen?" asked Miles.

"It's no friend of mine," she huffed.

Edgar gingerly scooped the bug into the jar and screwed on the lid. He examined it closely. "Unless I'm mistaken—which I doubt—this is a Botswallan wing-tipped rope eater."

"It doesn't mind toes so much, either," said Ellen, rubbing her foot.

"Yes, but they prefer fibrous materials," said Edgar. "Fabric, paper, et cetera. But they're also native to Botswalla, not Nod's Limbs. There's no way those ants accidentally ended up on the rope ladder. Someone put them there."

"The man in the paper-bag mask," said Ellen. "He tried to kill me!" She looked over the edge of the tree house, but the ground was completely shrouded by foliage.

"Quickly! We can still catch him," said Edgar. "To the ladder!"

"I hate to be Mr. Bad News," said Miles. "But what ladder?"

"Ack! We're trapped in this tree!" said Ellen. "*He's going to get away.* Well, we have no choice— Edgar, jump down there and go after him."

Edgar stuck his tongue out at his sister.

"We're not trapped," said Miles, opening a closet. "We can escape using Stephie's linens."

"There's no way a set of bed sheets will gets us down this tree," said Edgar.

"You know Stephie," said Miles. "She has more than a set of bed sheets up here. Way more."

So the twins and Pet and Miles set about making a new ladder from the diverse array of fabrics in the linen closet.

"By the time we're done, Bag Man will be miles away," grumbled Ellen as she tied a polka-dot bed sheet to a lace table runner.

"Don't worry," said Edgar, knotting a fringed throw rug to a crushed velvet curtain. "It's clear *he's* looking for *us*, too. We'll cross paths again."

Ellen pulled a pigtail. "When this whole election business is done, we are running some serious security drills at our house."

## 23. Role-y Poll-y

Election Day dawned bright and beautiful.

"The perfect day for a good vote," said Jill Geronimo, walking to Nod's Limbs Grammar School, her local polling place.

"It sure is!" said Marvin Matterhorn. "Eugenia Smithy is sure to win!"

"Really?" asked Jill, looking uncomfortable. "I read that nice weather favored a Blake Glide victory, on account of how mayoral he looks in sunglasses."

"But what about all this destructive pranking around town?" said Mrs. Elines. "Eugenia was right about that. I saw for myself the devastation in Old Town. Pure vandalism, I tell you!"

"You're all wrong," said Dr. McStern. "Nod is going to beat the pants off those other two. Rain or shine, he'll always be the founder of this town."

"Yes, it is charming to have your town founder still kicking after two centuries," Marvin Matterhorn retorted. "Too bad he's as screwy as a flying squirrel. Smithy stands for solidness, solidarity, and solid foods. None of that creamed corn nonsense. Makes us all soft."

"What's wrong with creamed corn?" asked Jill

Geronimo. "I love creamed corn! It's tasty and easy to digest. I bet Blake Glide is in favor of good digestion."

The argument continued all the way to the steps of the grammar school, where others were engaged in similar debate:

"No thanks to pranks! Elect Eugenia Smithy!"

"Help Nod's Limbs *glide* into a new era. Blake for Mayor!"

"Like cod? Vote Nod!"

This last came from the Society of Nod's Limbs Fishermen's Committee to Elect Nod for Mayor.

"This is crazy," said Ellen, as she and Edgar worked their way through the masses. Ellen wore a blond wig, glasses, and a flower-print dress. Edgar wore a top hat and tuxedo jacket with tails long enough to cover the bottoms of his footie pajamas.

"Crazy is good," said Edgar. "With all the hubbub, our plan should work smoothly. Ready?"

"All set."

The twins got in line with the rest of the voters. When they reached the front, Volunteer Election Judge Suzette Croquet asked for their names and addresses.

"I'm Georgia Peach," said Ellen in a Southern

accent, "from Alabama. I just moved here, and golly, do I like y'all's town! I can't wait to vote! I live at 442 Cairo Avenue."

"Welcome to Nod's Limbs, Ms. Peach," said Miss Croquet. "Hm, I don't see your name on the voter rolls—But heck, I don't want to be rude to a newcomer! Just fill this out and drop it in the box." She handed Ellen a ballot with boxes labeled EUGENIA SMITHY, BLAKE GLIDE, and AUGUSTUS NOD. Ellen didn't bother to step into the curtained voting booth. She boldy put a check next to Blake Glide's name and handed the ballot back.

"'Allo," said Edgar. "I am Sir Vondervear. I come to Nod's Limbs as diplomat from Vedgiestan. I vote in your election, no? I live at 1862 Vest Florence."

"The more the merrier!" said Suzette Croquet. "So many new faces in town—this must mean great things for Nod's Limbs!"

Edgar also placed a check next to Blake Glide, and the twins left the school. They scooted around back by the trash cans. Edgar pulled a walkie-talkie from his satchel.

"Breaker, breaker this is Striped Avenger. Come in, Shortstack."

Miles's voice crackled through the receiver.

"Roger, Striped Avenger, this is Shortstack. Can't I get a better name? I want to be Captain Muscles."

"Not now, Shortstack. What's your status?"

"All clear, sir. First vote accomplished at Town Hall. Commencing disguise change in T minus one minute."

Ellen leaned into the walkie's speaker. "Any sign of Bag Man, Miles? Anything suspicious at all?"

"Um, I don't know who this *Miles* is. I am *Shortstack*. And the answer is no. I'll keep you posted if I see something. Over and out!"

"Roger that, Shortstack. Keep up the good work." Edgar lowered the walkie-talkie and grinned at Ellen.

"You're ridiculous," she said.

"You're just mad because your code name is Smelly Footies," Edgar replied.

"What about Pet? How are we supposed to talk to it through a walkie-talkie?" Ellen asked.

"We worked out a system," said Edgar. He spoke into the receiver again. "Mighty Mop, come in, Mighty Mop."

A series of clicks echoed back. Edgar listened intently, nodding occasionally.

"Sounds good, Mighty Mop. Over and out." He clicked off the receiver.

"Morse code?" asked Ellen.

"Too easy to intercept," said Edgar. "This is my own alphanumeric cipher, based on the runic languages of ancient Scandinavia. *Norse* Code."

Ellen just snorted.

"Anyhow, Pet's staked out at the library. It had success as the lumberjack, and is changing into its bearded lady disguise."

"Excellent," said Ellen. "We should get moving. We have a lot of parts to play today."

And so the day continued, with Edgar, Ellen, Miles, and Pet switching costumes and voting as a

nurse, a deep-sea diver, a professional juggler, an astronaut, a spelunker, a dog-faced boy, a submarine captain, a dust-mop salesman, a sad clown, and a host of other people. Not once did anyone question their identities, and the plan went off without a hitch. As the hour neared six o'clock, closing time for the polls, the twins and their team regrouped again behind the school.

"Good work, everyone," said Edgar. "Nod is going to be a big loser, I can feel it."

"He'll be so proud," said Ellen.

## 24. Where Wolf?

*Beep, beep.*

A horn sounded from the driveway, and the conspirators peered around the corner of the school to see Bob pulling up in a mail truck. Miss Croquet emerged from the building, carrying a large box printed with VOTES: HIGHLY CONFIDENTIAL across the side.

"These are all of them," said Miss Croquet. "We had quite a turnout today, Interim Mayor. A lot of new faces, too. A wonderful showing of civic duty!"

"Communi-tee-riffic!" said Bob, opening the back of the truck and thrusting the box inside with five other similar-sized boxes.

"I heard there was some trouble with the votes at Town Hall," said Miss Croquet.

"Yes, unfortunately when one of our citizens came in to vote, he accidentally dropped a water balloon in the voters' box, and the ballots were soaked through. You can't see any check marks!"

Ellen jabbed Edgar in the chest. "Weren't *you* carrying a water balloon as part of your clown disguise?"

"I threw it at Mr. Poshi," said Edgar. "I didn't know it got on the votes!"

"Oh my, how terrible!" said Miss Croquet. "What are you going to do?"

"The only fair and square thing," said Bob. "I'm going to go door-to-door to every household in that district, and re-record all their votes by hand."

"That could take all night!" Miss Croquet gasped.

"It might," said Bob, "but as interim mayor, I have a duty to our citizens."

Edgar slapped his forehead.

"The concentration of our fake ballots was at

Town Hall," he said. "Without those, Nod could actually *win*."

"And whose fault is that?" said Ellen.

"I was *trying* to be authentic," Edgar replied.

"What do we do?" asked Miles.

"We're going to have to move to Plan B," said Ellen. "Bob is going door-to-door to ensure that box is one hundred percent genuine, so we need to get inside that truck and *over*stuff the other boxes with votes for Blake Glide."

"Where are we going to get the extra ballots, Sister?" Edgar asked.

"You're not the only one who thinks ahead, Brother," Ellen answered, producing a stack of fresh ballots from her pajamas. "I swiped them from the table when you were talking to Miss Croquet."

"Good thinking!" said Miles. "Okay, Pet and I will distract Bob while you guys get into the truck!"

Before either twin could stop their eager sidekick, Miles grabbed Pet and walked into the open. Miles inched closer to the interim mayor, who was loading the last box into the back of the truck.

"He better not blow this," whispered Edgar.

"It's Miles," said Ellen. "I'd say it's ninety percent blown."

Miles stood stock-still as Bob closed the back of the truck and then dug a key out of his pocket to lock it. Then, as if struck by a bolt of lightning, Miles shoved Pet under his shirt and howled like a beagle.

"Awoooooooooo!"

Edgar and Ellen hung their heads.

"So much for that," Ellen said.

But Bob the interim mayor looked up at the boy and stopped what he was doing.

"Hey, Miles," said Bob. "Did you just howl at me?"

"Um, Mr. Bob, I think you should get out of here," said Miles. "I've been bitten by a werewolf."

"Uh, a werewolf?" said Bob.

"Yes, one of the bloodthirsty creatures of the night whose bite passes a contagious condition known as lycanthropy—" began Miles.

"I know what a werewolf is," said Bob. "Are you sure it wasn't Mrs. Lentilberry's Chihuahua on the loose again?"

"No, I'm pretty sure it was a werewolf. I've seen the movies." Miles clutched his stomach where he'd stashed Pet and pretended to be nauseated. In the process, he managed to shove Pet up toward his collar. As a result, tufts of weird gray black-hair curled

out from his shirt. "Oooh, it's starting, Mr. Bob. I'm about to become a raging man-beast. Um, you should probably save yourself."

Miles fell on the ground and began howling like a coyote. He even scratched his ear with his foot for good measure.

"Well, Miles," said Bob. "Not only is it still daylight, but it's not even a full moon tonight. I should know: I'm a founding member of the Nod's Limbs Space-Gazers Club, and tonight is most definitely a waxing crescent."

"Really?" said Miles. "Gosh, Mr. Bob, I guess this must just be a sudden growth of chest hair. Thanks for setting me straight. I feel better already!"

"Any time, bucko," said Bob, as he turned back to the truck. "That's odd. I thought I had already closed this door. . . ."

## 25. Immortal Danger

"Wow. He really did it," said Edgar.

"You could knock me over with a teaspoon," agreed Ellen.

The twins ducked as Bob climbed into the driver's

seat and revved up the truck. He didn't notice two shadowy forms among the large boxes in the cargo bay. The engine rumbled with a hearty diesel growl, giving the twins plenty of cover to do their work.

"Let's get voting," said Ellen, handing Edgar a stack of ballots. The twins began filling them out as Bob made the rounds through the neighborhood, collecting people's replacement votes. For every Glide vote they cast, they reached inside a box and

pulled out a Nod vote. When it became apparent that most of the actual votes were for Nod, they started removing entire handfuls of ballots at a time, marveling at the near unanimous turnout for the old man.

Before long they had an enormous stack of Nod ballots to get rid of, but because they were locked inside the truck, they had nowhere to hide the evidence. When Bob stepped out of the truck to ring some doorbells, the twins did a little reconnaissance around the cargo bay, looking for a place to stash the votes.

Ellen was checking a nook behind the wheel well when her hand brushed something crinkly. She pulled out a paper bag.

"Tell me that was his lunch," said Edgar.

But when Ellen unfolded the bag, they saw that it had eye holes, and the same angry face they had seen in the sewers.

"Bob? Bob broke into our house? Took Nod's letters? Tailed us in the sewers? *Attempted insecticide on our persons?*"

"The evidence is right in front of us, Edgar," said Ellen. "His whole good-natured doofus persona is just an act. He's been out to get us from the start!"

"If it is really Bob—and that's an *if*—then he's far more cunning than we gave him credit for," said Edgar. "We could be in mortal danger."

"What could possibly be his motive for coming after us? I mean, really?"

"Maybe he's just crazy," suggested Edgar. "Crazy people don't need motives."

"Hm. That's plausible—at least where Bob is concerned."

"Shh, here he comes."

The twins stashed the bag and peered cautiously out the window that overlooked the driver's cab. They saw Bob climb into his seat, and wipe his brow.

"This night is really gonna be murder," he sighed.

The twins winced at each other in worry.

As Bob made the remainder of his rounds, Edgar looked for a means of escape. He rummaged in his satchel for his lock picking tools, but since the lock was on the other side of the door, his prized tumbler-cracking tweezers were useless. All they could do was hide in the shadows and wait.

Finally the truck rolled to a stop and the engine died. A key turned in the back door, and they ducked as Bob opened it. He pulled out the first big box of votes.

"Ooh! Democracy is so heavy!" He groaned.

As they heard his footsteps recede, the twins slipped out of the truck to safety. Edgar ran headfirst into some metal bars.

"What the—A cage? What kind of foul lair is this?"

"Cool it, genius, this isn't a cage for people. We're at . . ."

". . . the Nod's Limbs Zoo?" Edgar laughed. "Heh, these bars couldn't have contained me, anyway."

The twins slinked in the opposite direction from Bob and explored their surroundings.

"So the zoo is Bob's super-secret vote stashing location?" mused Ellen. "Smart, I guess. No one ever comes here."

This was true enough. For although the zoo boasted more than seventy different wild creatures on display, sixty-eight of them were animals most Nod's Limbsians could find in their own backyards, such as pigeons and petunia beetles. Most citizens made an obligatory once-a-year visit to the zoo, as an act of civic duty and local pride, but the spectacle of sixty-eight species of extraordinarily common animals failed to really solicit a sense of wonder in anyone but future zoologists, which in Nod's Limbs amounted only to Tad Von Barlow, son of the zoo director. And even though two of the seventy species qualified as mildly exotic, they failed to pack in the tourists. That's not hard to comprehend when one considers that the prized attractions were an albino chipmunk and a colony of—

"Botswallan wing-tipped rope eaters!" exclaimed Edgar. He pointed at a directory on the Hall of Insects, listing the notorious ant at the very top. "I didn't know the zoo had those."

"*Had*, indeed," said Ellen. She gestured to a sign on the door of the building:

BOTSWALLAN ROPE EATER DISPLAY
TEMPORARILY CLOSED

Beneath that was another sign:

WANTED: INFORMATION ON THE WHEREABOUTS
OF OUR BOTSWALLAN ROPE EATERS

"Egad! This is where Bob got them," Edgar said. "It's like this zoo is his supervillain fortress."

"I want to know what he's really up to," said Ellen. "Where do we snoop first?"

"The heart of his hideout, which will be some-place with real dramatic flair," said Edgar. "The best supervillains always have flair."

"You think Bob is one of the best supervillains?" asked Ellen. "Okay, well, there's the Mosquito Hatchery, the Squirrel Stables, and the Fun With Fungus Kiosk. Oh, and as you'll recall from last year's Operation: Souvenir and Yet so Far, the gift shop does double duty as the cafeteria."

"Gift shop," said Edgar. "That's appropriately quirky."

The gift shop was unlocked, and the twins let themselves in. They peered into the darkness, hoping to find some incriminating master plan written on blueprints, or perhaps a videotape of Bob explaining his vendetta against his archenemies (as supervillains sometimes do). But all they found were racks of novelty antlers and bunny-shaped cake plates.

"I wonder where he put it?" asked Edgar.

"Put what?" said a voice as the lights clicked on. Bob stood in the doorway, holding a crowbar.

## 26. The Price of Democracy

"Gahh!" shouted the twins.

"I mean—Oh, Bob. There you are," said Ellen. "We were just doing a security check. We heard there were some mischief makers about, trying to rig the election."

"Ha, ha, that's a good one, Ellen." Bob laughed. "You're always ready with a good cover story. Rule number four in your How to Pull a Prank checklist."

"Right. Number four." Ellen sighed.

"All right, no more charades," said Edgar. "You won't take us without a fight, you backstabber. What have you got against us, anyway?"

"Hey, hey now, it's nothing personal," said Bob. "I knew you two would try to prank the election, just like the others."

"The others?"

"You can come out now!" Bob called out. "Ms. Smithy! Mr. Glide! The game's up!"

There was a rustle, and Eugenia Smithy emerged from under the lemon slush machine.

"You too, Mr. Glide!"

"Mr. Glide isn't here right now," a voice said from the fuzzy gopher keychain display.

"Then who's talking to me?" asked Bob.

"Darn it," said Blake Glide, and he lumbered out from the keychains.

"Good pranking, all of you," said Bob. "But I figured it out! You can't put one over on Bob, interim mayor!"

"What the heck are you talking about?" said Edgar.

"Your clever attempts to spice up our civic contest," said Bob. "I've been tiptoeing after all of you as you tiptoed after one another, and I salute each of you for the great effort to make this our prankiest election ever. I hate to be the party pooper, but it is my job to make sure we have a fair and square race."

"But . . . but . . . you're the man in the paper-bag mask!" said Edgar.

"Ooh, is that you?" asked Blake Glide. "You know, I'm looking for my next role. . . ."

"It's true," said Bob with a chuckle. "I did hide my signature good looks with a snazzy disguise."

"Then you admit you're a thief and a tried-to-murder-us murderer!" cried Ellen.

"Ha! Rule number five: Attempt to confuse the authorities when caught," said Bob. "Nice try again, Ellen. Nope, I may be crazy about our pranks, but

I'm even crazier about democracy! I've just been keeping tabs on all of you as you tried to outmischief one another. Big fun!"

Edgar leaned toward his sister. "I'm starting to think Bob isn't our rival."

"Then who *is*?" asked Ellen.

Eugenia Smithy tapped her foot impatiently.

"What about the votes, then?" she asked. "Am I right in thinking that we *all* stuffed the boxes?"

"You're kidding me," said Ellen.

"It's true!" said Bob. "Ms. Smithy just swapped out the Old Town ballot box with one of her own, and Mr. Glide was about to start lowering fake ballots into the boxes using a fishing pole. Am I right?"

Blake Glide pulled a rod and reel from the keychain display and waved it meekly.

The twins smacked their heads in disbelief.

"Not to worry!" said Bob. "I have a complete voter registry. All I have to do is compare the votes to the names on this list, and separate the real ones from the fake ones."

"There are *thousands* of votes," said Eugenia.

"I know. Good thing I have all night, huh?" said Bob.

"Well, better get going, then," said Blake Glide.

"Thanks for being so understanding about this, Bob. You're a good man. No need to involve the police, I say."

"Why would I call the police for a prank?" asked Bob.

"No reason, no reason," said Blake Glide. "Come on, all, let's go. Fun's over. See you tomorrow for the count."

Blake Glide headed to the exit, followed by Eugenia Smithy and the twins. Bob barred the door after them with the crowbar.

As they left, Ellen turned to Edgar.

"Nod is going to kill us."

They hung their heads and sang:

> *O horrid day! We've botched the job—*
> *Been one step behind Intern Bob.*
> *The whole affair makes our heads throb,*
> *And that's just the beginning.*
> *It's been all "Hurry!" "Hie!" and "Haste!"*
> *But all of it has been a waste,*
> *And Nod will blow his stack when faced*
> *With the prospect of winning.*

## 27. The Count

By eight o'clock the next morning, Founder's Park was packed. Nod's Limbsians had brought out their beach blankets, lawn chairs, and picnic baskets, and hardly a square inch of grass wasn't occupied.

The twins walked glumly into the fray, fearing the inevitable. Pet was so sullen, it refused to come out of Edgar's satchel.

"I can't believe you didn't tell Nod what happened," Ellen said.

"Me? I didn't hear *you* shouting it from the rafters," Edgar replied.

"How do you break the news to someone that he's been elected mayor?" said Ellen. "That's like having your child elected class president."

"Devastating," agreed Edgar. "You never know. Maybe he lost, after all."

As they neared the park, they saw Blake Glide and Eugenia Smithy standing on a stage where the counting would take place. They both looked tense. The twins felt a hand on each of their shoulders.

"There you are," said Bob. "We're almost ready. I'm having the candidates stand onstage with me while I count out the votes. Where's Nod? Is he on his way?"

"Uh, he sent us as his emissaries," said Ellen. "He woke up this morning with a flesh-eating bacteria. Nothing too serious, but he didn't want to spread it to the populace, just in case it's contagious."

"What a thoughtful man!" said Bob. "He will make a generous leader, if he turns out to be the winner." Bob winked at the twins. "As his representatives, then, won't you join me and the other candidates?"

The twins followed Bob to the platform.

"Flesh-eating bacteria?" Edgar whispered.

"I'm setting the stage for an untimely death," she whispered back. "Or at least severe quarantine. You can't be mayor if you can't be grand marshal in parades."

"At least not in this town."

Bob took the stage and the twins joined Eugenia and Blake Glide. Eugenia wrung her hands nervously.

"I wanted to apologize to each of you," she said. "I let this election go too far. I'm not the kind of person who cheats. At least, not on a civic level like this." She eyed the twins guiltily. "Being mayor isn't worth turning the electoral process into a farce, and I'm sorry."

"I'm sorry too," said Blake Glide. "If I lose, so be

it. Besides, as mayor, how could I fulfill my dream of being a renegade cop who always defies the police commissioner to bring down the bad guys, often laying waste to the city with overly long car-chase sequences and unnecessary explosions? Mayor would really limit my range."

The twins and Eugenia stared blankly at Blake Glide.

"Right," Eugenia said finally. "At any rate, I'm glad this will be a fair race. May the best Nod's Limbsian win."

"Or out-of-town, soon-to-be citizen," said Blake Glide.

The large speakers on either side of the stage blared to life. Bob's voice echoed across the park.

"Welcome, Nod's Limbsians, to our first of many Vote-Counting-a-Thons! We will soon know the results of this election, and I'd just like to applaud our worthy candidates, who throughout it all showed themselves to be true citizens of this town!"

The crowd cheered, and Blake Glide bowed.

"Before we begin," Bob continued, "I'd just like to say how honored I am to have served as your interim mayor during the last few months. And now, to the votes!"

Applause and merriment erupted from the crowd as Bob hoisted a large crate onto the stage.

"In this box are thousands of eligible votes. Let's get count-a-thoning!"

Bob stuck a crowbar into the top of the crate and wrenched it off.

*"Aiiieee!"* he shrieked as a wave of rats surged out of the crate, knocking him to the ground and flooding into the park. Cheers turned to screams and picnics to panic as the rats swarmed the townspeople, who tried in vain to protect their egg-salad sandwiches and thermoses of lemonade. And these were no ordinary rats. It appeared that their gray fur had been painted with *red stripes*, looking very much like a certain duo's footie pajamas.

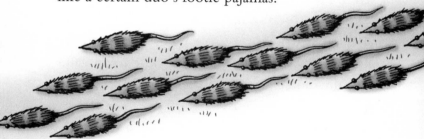

Edgar and Ellen glanced at each other.

"Did you do this?"

"I wish. You?"

"Nope."

"Hm."

The twins looked at Edgar's satchel, where Pet lay hiding. There had been an instance the previous year in which Pet had shown its ability to communicate with rats, and had let them loose on the twins as payback for so many years of torment.

"Pet? Was this your idea?"

Pet popped out of the satchel and shook its eyeball no. It shrugged its tendrils.

"Then who—" Ellen began, but Bob interrupted her.

"Really, Edgar and Ellen, was that necessary? I mean, I'm all for a good prank, but I thought I explained last night that this day was too important. . . ."

"Yeah," said Blake Glide. "What gives? I thought we said no cheating, er, pranking."

"Yes, this was going too far," said Eugenia Smithy.

"I swear, we didn't do this," said Edgar. Ellen, however, frowned at her accusers.

"But what if we did?" she demanded, turning to face the crowd. "What if we did prank the election? It's what we *do*! It's what we always did for years, and none of you ever noticed! You blamed our tricks on the weather, or the Earth's gravitational pull, or just plain bad luck. *We were behind everything.* And then you made us into heroes, and you know what happened? We went soft! We didn't ruin the debate or unleash these rats, but we should have! The old us *would* have! But we've turned goody-goody!" Ellen paused. Hundreds of eyes blinked at her. "We've turned into one of you, and it makes me sick."

The crowd stood silent. Finally little Annie Krump spoke up, her voice small but strong.

"You're not very nice."

The words resonated with the townspeople, who began to echo the sentiment:

"Yeah, not very nice at all."

"Downright mean, in fact."

Other voices chimed in:

"What's wrong with being goody-goody? Isn't goody good?"

"Seems inherent in the name."

"Who doesn't want to be good?"

"Edgar and Ellen, that's who!" cried Agnes of the Old Town Action Committee. "If they don't respect signs, what *do* they respect?"

"Nothing!" cried the Supreme Hoo-ha of the Royal Kerfuffle. "They don't like hats, and they don't like *us*!"

The crowd turned on the twins, who had never seen such disgust in the Nod's Limbsians' eyes. Even the Edgar and Ellen Fan Club, each member fighting back tears, had tossed aside their striped pajamas and hidden themselves in shame under picnic blankets.

Bob looked at them gravely.

"I think you two should leave."

"Fine!" said Ellen.

"Don't have to ask us twice!" said Edgar.

The twins marched off the stage toward the park exit. A half-eaten banana hit Edgar in the cheek. A glop of potato salad followed, landing square on Ellen's head. Soon the twins were running for home, dodging the barrage of picnic foodstuffs the Nod's Limbsians pelted at them.

# 28. The Trappings of Failure

"Well, everybody pretty much hates us now," said Edgar. He dunked Pet into a tub of vinegar and used the creature to scrub the crusted egg salad loose from his pajamas. Pet didn't seem to mind.

"That's okay, isn't it?" asked Ellen, swinging idly from the ballroom chandelier. "Doesn't that mean everything's back to normal?"

"Not really. You said it yourself: No one in this town used to even acknowledge us. Now they know who we are, and they despise us."

This left Ellen quiet for some time. Then she said, "Well, we despised them first. So there."

"I'm just saying things are never going to be 'back to normal,'" said Edgar.

"Not *everyone* hates you, children," said Nod. The old man wandered into the ballroom, twirling a tin flute. "I'm grateful for your efforts to keep city officials off my doorstep. Even if the rats weren't your handiwork, you still acted for the greater good. Although no one may ever know it."

"They'll be back, Nod," said Ellen. "There's bound to be another election."

Nod tootled a few notes on his flute, then looked

up absently. "No worries. By then, I'll be long gone."

"Gone?" cried the twins.

"Hm?" Nod asked.

"Gone? Where are you going?" asked Ellen.

"Oh, dear, did I say that aloud?" Nod fidgeted. "Phooey. Well, I suppose I should tell you anyway. Children, the time is coming to stop working in theory and begin working in practice. My experiments have gone as far as they can here. Next I'll need to travel to the other balm springs to collect samples."

"What do you hope to prove?" asked Edgar.

"I hope to prove that my calculations are wrong," said Nod. "If not, we could be in serious trouble."

"Trouble how? What's your big secret about?" asked Ellen.

Nod twirled the flute again several times. "The balm is a monstrosity. Oh, it kept me alive, and it sustains old Pilosoculus, sure. But make no mistake: Once man is touched with the greed for it, he'll stop at nothing to get more."

"Mad Duke Disease," said Ellen. "The circus folk told us about it."

"That's just the effect of *one* balm," said Nod. "Combine two or three different types and . . . Well, there are more things in Heaven and Earth,

Ellen, than are dreamt of in your philosophy."

"He's quoting Shakespeare again, Edgar," said Ellen.

"In order to sound meaningful without really saying anything," said Edgar. "We know your tricks, Nod."

"Really?" he asked. "What about the one where I use this flute as a pea shooter to blow a stink bomb into your ear, boy?"

"You wouldn't—"

*Paff!*

As the twins waved the clouds of green gas away, Nod rolled on the floor laughing.

"Grow—*kaff, kaff*—up, Nod!" wheezed Edgar.

"Never!" The old man laughed.

The sound of a submarine's claxon cut their revelry short.

*Ah-WOOOga! Ah-WOOOga!*

"That's the Merrimack Attack!" cried Ellen. "The fifth-floor saltwater taffy trap!"

"Our intruder is back," sneered Edgar. "And this time he can expect a nastier reception!"

"After him, my striped avengers!" called Nod as the twins dashed for the elevator, Pet bouncing after them. They slid down the elevator cables to the fifth floor and ran straight into a wad of blue taffy stretched across the corridor.

"He seems to have escaped the taffy trap," said Edgar, pulling himself free of the gummy blue goo. "He might be heading toward the—"

*Whoop, whoop, whoop, whoop, whoop!*

"—the Whooping Coffin," said Ellen. "Next floor down. Go!"

The twins and Pet ran down the stairs toward the incessant whooping alarm, and sure enough, the trap had been sprung. Just as the twins had designed it, the pine coffin had fallen from the ceiling and clamped its lid shut. The twins threw open the lid.

"We've got you now—" began Edgar. "Er, we would . . . if you hadn't gotten away."

"Empty? It must have just missed him," said Ellen. "But he's heading downward, which means he may yet trip the Slay-bell Sluice."

The sound of another alarm came as if in answer: *Jingle, jingle, jingle!*

"The sluice it is!" called Edgar. The staircase to the third floor had collapsed into a flat, smooth chute. Water gushed from a fire hose, turning the staircase into a sloshing river. Edgar and Ellen grabbed a hidden inner tube from under a divan and

rode the slide whitewater style. Pet paddled ahead of them on a boat of its own hair.

"This flows all the way to the basement," said Edgar. "The tuna net should collect anyone who got flushed down the sluice."

"I'm going to mount this particular fish on our wall, Brother," said Ellen.

When they washed into the basement, Edgar steered them to the side of the massive tuna net that lay in wait. But while the twins had deftly avoided the net's snare, so had their intruder. The net lay empty, save for a waterlogged Pet.

"He's nimble, I'll give him that," said Edgar.

"He's making for the sewer," said Ellen. "Sub-basement. Now!"

They dashed down another flight of stairs, where they saw that the spring-loaded wall had been opened.

Pet slipped down the dirt tunnel, and the twins wriggled down after it. They were just emerging into the sewer tunnel when they heard a muffled *ga-wump*.

"Another trap sprung," said Edgar. "Do you think he avoided it?"

But when the twins turned the corner, they

saw Pet jumping up and down on a length of air-conditioning ductwork from which jutted a pair of sneakers. It was the snag-and-bag trap, and it had finally caught their quarry.

Ellen gave the shoes a yank, and Miles Knightleigh spilled out of the trap.

"Miles? You dirty sneak!" she growled.

"What were you doing messing around with us like that?" demanded Edgar.

"I thought I was drilling," said Miles. "Like you said back in the tree house, Ellen. We were going to run some security drills after the election."

"For Nod's sake, wait for me to give the order next time," said Edgar.

"But you did," said Miles.

"What?"

"It's right here in this note," said Miles, unfurling a scrap of paper from his pocket. "It's one of your secret messages. Did I use the decoder ring wrong?"

"Let me see that," said Edgar, swiping the paper. Indeed, the scrap was covered with the bizarre scrawls and symbols of Edgar's creation. "Yes, these are my codes all right, but . . ."

As Edgar read the decoded message at the bottom, his eyes grew wide:

*Private Miles—*

*Time to test our defenses! At exactly 7:00 this
evening, I want you to set off all the traps in
the house from the fifth floor on down. Can you
trip each one without getting caught? Ellen and
I will pursue. . . . Do not let us catch you! Keep
running, and we'll see how ready we are to repel
an intruder.*

*—Commander Edgar*

"I sent no such note," said Edgar.

"Ha, ha! That's a pranky prank, Ellen." Miles
laughed.

"I pulled no such prank," said Ellen.

"You mean," began Edgar, "that we've just followed a wild-goose chase into the sewers . . ."

". . . and left our house defenseless?" finished
Ellen.

"We've been duped!" said the twins, and they
spun on their heels and raced off toward their house.

## 29. The Culprit Found

"I can't believe we were so foolish!" cried Ellen as they dashed from the basement into the foyer. Although the front door was open, nothing else seemed amiss. Edgar's satchel shrine was untouched, the bust of Poe sat where it should, and all was quiet.

"Nod?" Edgar called out, but there was no answer. Miles and Pet joined them as they scouted each floor for signs of an intruder. But there was nothing—no dirty footprints, no shattered knick-knacks, no rifled-through drawers.

Nothing, that is, until the fifth floor.

Pet reached the landing first. The twins saw it shudder and bolt down the corridor.

"Pet, wait, what is it?" Ellen called, sprinting up the last few steps, Edgar and Miles just behind her. She gasped when she gained the landing. Farther down the hallway, a body lay across the doorway to Nod's office. Pet sat beside the shaggy gray head, stroking the forehead with a tendril.

"Oh no, Nod," said Ellen, running up. She examined his face while Edgar put his ear to Nod's chest.

"I can hear a heartbeat," he said.

"Who would do this?" asked Ellen.

"She would!" shouted Miles, pointing into the office. The twins turned in time to see Stephanie Knightleigh jump up onto the windowsill.

"Stephanie!" cried the twins.

"Hello, old friends," said Stephanie, malice dripping from her voice. Neither Edgar nor Ellen had seen their archnemesis in person since that fateful day when their house had collapsed, and even the sight of her on television could not prepare them for what she looked like now.

She wore neither a frilly, purple dress nor an itchy, gray school uniform, but an entirely black ensemble, from turtleneck to boots. Slung over one shoulder was a backpack full of Nod's beakers, vials, and notebooks. Her normally bouncy red curls were pulled back into a ponytail. But the scowl she turned on the twins was familiar enough.

"What have you done to Nod?" Ellen demanded.

"And why did you break into our house?" asked Miles.

"And what are you wearing?" said Edgar.

Stephanie tossed her ponytail playfully.

"I knocked him unconscious; because I needed something here; and a new look I'm trying out. Like it?" Stephanie posed, modeling her new duds.

"But we saw you get on that boat!" said Edgar.

"It's amazing how hard and fast you can swim when you see the land of your rightful mayorship disappearing on the horizon," said Stephanie.

"Put down Nod's things, Stephanie," Ellen said.

"Or you'll do what?" Stephanie shot back. "*Nothing*, that's what. I've broken into your house *twice,* turned the town against you, attacked you with ants, and even successfully pranked the election when you failed to. You're obviously no threat to me. And you never were."

"You know nothing about the balm," said Edgar. "You've never even seen it."

Stephanie looked at them with mock pity. "Really? Ellen came out of the balm spring with two buckets of goop. Didn't you notice you had only one when the dust settled?"

"You stole that bucket!" cried Ellen. "It wasn't destroyed at all!"

"That stuff's dangerous," said Edgar. "You're in way over your head."

"Now that I have Nod's goodies, I've got a pretty good handle on it, thanks," Stephanie replied. "Enough chat. I'm glad I had a chance to humiliate you while I was in town. Now if you'll excuse me, I have a brilliant master plan to enact."

"Give me Nod's stuff, ex-princess," demanded Ellen.

Stephanie dangled the journal out the window. "Come and fetch it, dogbreath."

Ellen charged at her rival at top speed, but before she could make contact, there was a *flash* and a *bang* and a puff of black smoke filled the room. Ellen sailed through the cloud, clutching for Stephanie. What she got instead was the breeze outside the window. If Edgar hadn't grabbed her by the footie at the last moment, she would have dived clean out the window. They fanned the smoke away, coughing.

"Did she fall to a grisly death?" asked Ellen.

When they looked down, it was not the broken body of their foe they saw, but a deflated parachute.

"No kidding, she jumped," said Edgar, his voice just slightly tinged with awe.

They heard a motor scooter roar to life and saw Stephanie pull away in a cloud of dust.

"She's got Nod's journal!" cried Ellen. "All his notes, all his writings on the balm! Quick, after Stephanie!"

*"Quick, after Ronan!"* shouted a voice behind them.

Edgar, Ellen, Miles, and Pet all turned. Standing beside Nod's body in the doorway was a ragged woman with ripped clothes and wild hair. If not for the dark, familiar eyes burning beneath her filthy face, Ellen would not have recognized her.

## 30. The Green-eyed Monster

"Dahlia!"

Ellen raced to her. Before she reached the shockingly haggard Dahlia, the woman nearly collapsed from exhaustion. Only the doorframe kept her upright.

"Miles, get some water!"

"Right away!"

"Edgar, help Nod! I'll put Dahlia on the couch to rest!"

"No," Dahlia said. "Is no time to rest, Ellen."

Edgar kneeled next to Nod and placed his satchel beneath the man's head. Pet continued to brush Nod's cheeks until the two wrinkled eyes fluttered and opened.

"What . . . ?" Nod winced, reaching a hand to the back of his head. "*Oooh* . . . that smarts . . ."

"Easy, Nod," Edgar said softly. "You were attacked."

"I know that," Nod said. "I was there when it happened."

Edgar eased Nod back to his feet, and Ellen helped Dahlia into Nod's office. Pet sat dutifully on his old friend's shoulder.

"It must have been a heck of a hit—Ellen, you almost look like Dahlia to these whoozy eyes."

Dahlia's voice broke as she sunk into the office leather couch. "Oh, Augustus, he is gone! They are all gone! All of them—the whole family. Missing!"

"What?" said Nod. "Can't be, can't be . . ."

"Yes." Dahlia brushed tears from her soiled cheeks. "We thought our moonhoney would be for making peace with our family. To seek Benedict and mend broken trust. But when we come to Bavaria . . . ," Dahlia paused. "We find only abandoned circus tents and empty Ferris wheel, spinning and spinning."

"Where did they all go?"

"We found only one trail into wood—a trail of many, many footprints. We follow for some time, but the traces, they disappeared at a river. No clue remained to guide us, not even a wad of the cottoned candy or a stray peanut."

"A whole circus gone?" marveled Nod. "Dahlia, where is Ronan now?"

"He is following hunch to go east," she said. "He heads for another balm spring. I want to go with him, but he insist I come here to warn you."

Edgar cracked his knuckles. "First, Stephanie goes after Nod's balm experiments. . . . Then the balm's protectors go missing. This can't possibly be a coincidence can it?"

"Stephanie?" Nod exclaimed. "A *Knightleigh* did this to me?" He leaped up with the vigor of a man half his age (even if a man half his age was more than a hundred years old. Regardless, it was vigorous, indeed).

"Hi!" said Miles, running into the office with a tall glass of water. "I'm a Knightleigh!"

"I knew a Knightleigh would be tied up in this!" Nod bellowed. "There's no one more tainted by greed. That Stephanie is the worst of all of them!"

"She's a stinker," said Miles. "She makes me want to change my last name. I like Gustafson. Miles Gustafson. You like how that sounds, Edgar?"

"Nod, you should also know . . . she apparently has her own bucket of balm," said Ellen.

Nod groaned. He pulled a dusty globe from the top of his bookshelf and gave it a spin. "Miss Knightleigh has my experiments, my data, and enough balm to experiment with." He sighed. "She is a threat. Whether she is tied to the disappearance of the circus I cannot say, but this much I know: Things must be set right, and only we remain to do it."

Ellen halted the spinning globe with her finger. "So what's the plan, Nod?"

"Dahlia, you returned with the blimp, I surmise?"

"Is docked above us, Augustus, and ready to launch."

"Then Dahlia and I go after the circus," said Nod. "We begin in Bavaria and follow our own hunches from there. Edgar and Ellen? You will track down the rottenest Knightleigh and retrieve her balm bucket and my equipment."

Nod strode toward the elevator almost faster than anyone could keep up. As they rode to the roof, he barked commands like a field general.

"Pilosoculus? Look after these children. Do not touch any balm yourselves, not even you, Pilos. If captured, do not reveal any information about our half of this plan, is that clear? We will meet you here as soon as our mission is complete."

On the roof, Nod and Dahlia ascended the ladder steps to the blimp cockpit. The old man took one last look across the landscape of the town he had founded.

"I have wasted enough time here," he said. "Elections and muffins and mayors and whatever else. Bah to all of it! It is long past time for me to leave. And so, young ones, I wish you success. I shall miss you. If we never meet again, please know that your presence in my old age has warmed the cookies of my heart."

"Uh, I think you mean the *cockles* of your heart," said Edgar.

"No, I meant cookies," said Nod with a smile. "Cheerio, you lovable little chuckleheads!"

And with that he loosed the tether and closed the cockpit hatch.

"Stay safe, little ones!" called Dahlia.

A moment later the blimp was soaring off into the distance, someplace east of Nod's Limbs. The twins, Pet, and Miles watched as it disappeared into the ether.

## 31. Not So Hard to Say Good-bye

"Where do we begin?" asked Edgar. They had returned to Nod's office, where Ellen was rummaging through the remaining papers on Nod's desk.

"Help me sort through these papers," said Ellen. "Something here might provide a clue."

Pet dipped a tendril into the pot of ink on the desk and swirled a coded message across the wooden surface: *"Recall, my twins, the maps in letters wrote: It was far north that Benedict did note."*

"That's true," said Edgar. "He mentioned the Black Diamond Glacier in one letter."

"Nod kept talking about replicating cold conditions to work with the balm. If Stephanie is using his notes as a guide . . . ," began Ellen. She pulled an old world

map off the wall that had a few circled locations—one was labeled BLACK DIAMOND. She rolled up the map and tucked it into Edgar's satchel.

"So we're really doing this, eh? Leaving Nod's Limbs?" said Edgar. "You know, we've never been farther than the 'Welcome to Nod's Limbs' sign on the eastern edge of town."

Ellen looked out the window at peaceful Nod's Limbs. "What's to miss about this place? We're exposed, universally reviled . . . I can't think of anything I'd rather be doing than ditching this town and hunting for Stephanie. Plus, you know . . . the fate of humanity in the balance and all that . . ."

Edgar nodded. "Time to fire up the balloon, then?"

Miles looked from Edgar to Ellen. "All right! Vacation!"

"Uh, no, Miles," said Ellen. "This is a twin-only journey. And their pet."

"But why not?" asked Miles. "We're the perfect team, guys! Edgar's the vanilla and you're the chocolate and I'm the cherry on top of this great, big ice-cream sundae of teamwork!"

"Wouldn't Pet be the cherry? What with the one eye and everything . . ." said Edgar.

Ellen glared at him. "You all are giving me an ice-cream headache. There is no great, big sundae. We go alone, Miles. You can look after yourself right here, can't you?"

Before Edgar turned to go, he noticed Miles's hurt look.

"Actually," Edgar said smoothly, "there *is* a great big sundae, Miles. And you're the candied nuts. But these nuts have to stay behind in town to keep watch in case Nod returns. Then you'd have to contact the rest of the sundae."

"Oh, I'm nuts!" said Miles, perking up. "I can be nuts!"

And so, Edgar prepared the balloon as Ellen stocked it with food, blankets, winter hats, power tools, some assorted sprockets and springs, and Nod's remaining paperwork. Pet plotted the route on the map, although directions appeared sketchy at best. They could only be assured they were headed north.

Shortly after sunrise, they were packed and as ready as they could be. The twins and Pet trundled into the balloon's basket, and Edgar fired up the burner. Ellen cut the rope tying them to the ground, and like that, they were off. Miles waved from the grass below, running after them as they floated away.

"Have a safe trip! Don't forget to write! Send me a penguin friend!" he called after them.

"Make sure you water Morella and Gustav every day!" shouted Ellen in reply. "And sour milk—they love sour milk!"

Edgar gazed at the horizon, stretched out before them like multicolored taffy.

"Good riddance, Nod's Limbs," said Edgar.

"Look out, world," Ellen replied. With that, the twins sang a song in tremulous voices:

> *The future is a fickle brute.*
> *It probably thinks that it's a hoot*
> *To send us off in cold pursuit*
> *Along this vaguely northern route.*
> *We'll go where others fear to tread,*
> *Across that sky so fiery red—*
> *A warning of some future dread*
> *Or welcome to the world ahead?*
> *Good-bye, Nod's Limbs, we've fiends to track,*
> *And miles to go ere we come back.*

Pet nodded its eyeball as the clock tower struck seven. The good citizens of Nod's Limbs would at this moment exit their homes, headed to their offices and shops to begin a day of predictable work. They would carry predictable sandwiches in their lunchboxes and drive predictable routes to their destinations.

And, predictably, not a single one of them would bother to look skyward as the hot-air balloon piloted by two children in striped pajamas sailed silently above their heads, a gentle wind at its back and a promise of something unpredictable ahead.

THE END

# Edgar & Ellen

# Frost Bites

EDGAR AND ELLEN PURSUE STEPHANIE TO THE FRIGID north, only to find that she isn't the worst of their worries. Something lives on the slopes of the Glöggen-heim, something that doesn't take kindly to being disturbed. What wonders await the twins in this wintry wasteland? And what does rendered blubber have to do with it?

BOOK 8 OF THE EDGAR & ELLEN SERIES

## Coming Soon!

WWW.EDGARANDELLEN.COM

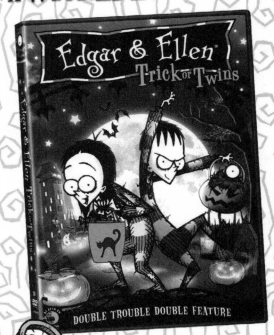

### BOOK 1
# Edgar & Ellen: Rare Beasts
Edgar and Ellen dream BIG when it comes to pranks. After they learn that exotic animals are worth tons of money, the twins devise a get-rich-quick scheme that sends Nod's Limbs into a frenzy!

### BOOK 2
# Edgar & Ellen: Tourist Trap
Mayor Knightleigh wants to turn little Nod's Limbs into a premiere vacation destination. But Edgar and Ellen have a plan to give the too-sweet townspeople all the attention they deserve!

### BOOK 3
# Edgar & Ellen: Under Town
Someone is causing a lot of trouble in town, but it isn't Edgar and Ellen! To catch this new mischievous miscreant, the twins must scour the sewers and uncover someone's dirty secret.

Add to the adventure at www.edgarandellen.com!

BOOK 4
## Edgar & Ellen: Pet's Revenge
Intruders invade the twins' house! But just when they need to stand together, one twin takes a sudden interest in... *niceness*? Now it's twin against twin, and somehow Pet is to blame.

BOOK 5
## Edgar & Ellen: High Wire
A bizarre circus appears in the dead of night, and the twins try to join. They hope to skip town and escape the wrath of Heimertz. But nothing at a circus is ever as it seems...

BOOK 6
## Edgar & Ellen: Nod's Limbs
Augustus Nod has launched a treasure hunt from beyond the grave! The twins must solve the riddles and discover Nod's lost golden limbs before the Knightleighs bury the past—and the twins with it!

# HELP! MISSING AUTHOR!

CHARLES OGDEN, AVID CAMPER, FISHERMAN, BUG COLLECTOR, AND AUTHOR OF THE EDGAR & ELLEN SERIES, HAS GONE MISSING! THOUGH OGDEN IS KNOWN TO BE AN ERRATIC, UNPREDICTABLE PERSONALITY, WE HAVE NEVER HAD A PROBLEM RETRIEVING HIS MANUSCRIPTS FROM THE SECRET LOCATIONS HE CHOOSES TO LEAVE THEM.

BUT WHEN WE RECENTLY WENT TO THE TRASH CAN BEHIND THE TAS-TEE SERV ICE-CREAM PARLOR IN WEST PENNYFARTHING, WE DID NOT FIND THE DRAFT TO BOOK 8 AS OGDEN HAD PROMISED. INSTEAD, WE FOUND ONLY A SCRAP OF PAPER WITH THE WORDS "OTTER'S FIBS" SCRAWLED UPON IT. AND NOW OGDEN IS NOT RESPONDING TO THE USUAL SMOKE SIGNALS, HOMING RAVENS, AND HIGHWAY BILLBOARDS WE USE TO COMMUNICATE WITH HIM.

CLEARLY, WE NEED YOUR HELP. LOG ON TO WWW.EDGARANDELLEN.COM/MISSINGAUTHOR AND FOLLOW THE INSTRUCTIONS TO SOLVE THIS MYSTERY.

# COMING SOON!

## OTTER'S FIBS

What? This CAN'T be the name of the next book. It's too weird, even for Edgar and Ellen! But this is the only clue given to us by Charles Ogden—and we can't find him . . . OR the manuscript for the next book!

Help us find the author and his next book, or else the Edgar & Ellen series is doomed!

Turn the page to join the hunt.

Sincere thanks,
The Publisher

Charles Ogden *is an avid camper and fisherman. He collects insects and has traveled in pursuit of various specimens to the North Pole, the South Pole, and Poland. Mr. Ogden and his insect collection make their home in a cool, dry, preservation-friendly environment, far removed from prying eyes.*

Rick Carton *has been drawing longer than he's been walking. In his Chicago studio he has a cherished collection of every pencil ever worn down to a nub during his lengthy artistic career. He has never formally studied art; instead, the art community has diligently studied him. They are yet to release their findings.*